Christmas
UNWRAPPED

Christmas Unwrapped

Copyright © 2022,2023 by C L Easton

All rights reserved.

No part of this publication may be reproduced, distributed, or transmitted in any form or by any means, including photocopying, recording, or other electronic or mechanical methods, without the prior written permission of the author, except in the case of brief quotations embodied in critical reviews and certain other non-commercial uses permitted by copyright law.
Please note the spelling throughout is Canadian English.

Cover Design: Black Pirate Book Cover

Publisher: Black Rose Publishing

Paperback Alternative ISBN: 978-1-998910-06-9

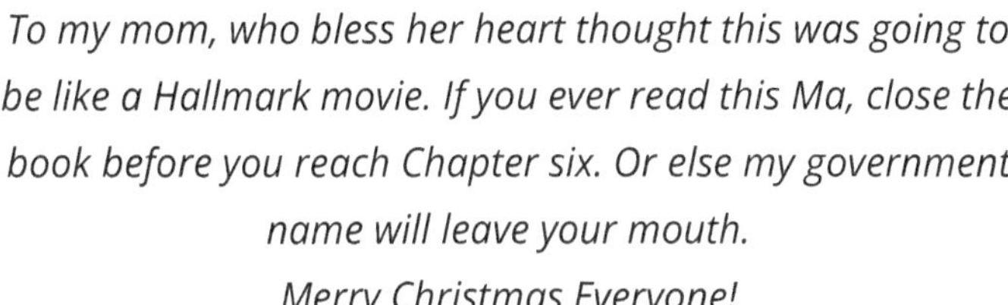

To my mom, who bless her heart thought this was going to be like a Hallmark movie. If you ever read this Ma, close the book before you reach Chapter six. Or else my government name will leave your mouth.

Merry Christmas Everyone!

1

Noel

Christmas is supposed to be the best time of the year. Yet I'm stuck in this cabin, snowed in. Now you're probably asking yourself, Noel, how the hell did that happen? I'll set the scene for you.

Mountains, snowstorm, and I didn't check the goddamn weather.

Four days until Christmas, I came to this cabin to relax, if you were also wondering. Probably not. I don't blame you. My life became rather complicated earlier this week when I walked in on my boyfriend and my best friend. I did the only rational thing and slashed all the tires on both of their vehicles before leaving town because it was either the tires or them, and I don't look good in orange.

I won't lie. The view up here is nice; I only wish I could enjoy it from outside. The cabin I have is rustic, like cut your own wood for heat, rustic. I do have running water, so that's a bonus. The fireplace is my favourite piece. It's floor-to-ceiling stone, with a dark solid timber beam for the mantle. The ceiling beams are exposed, making the cabin seem more significant than it is. Honestly, this entire place is beautiful. The snow that is piling up against the front door, on the other hand? Nope.

I'm mixing my hot chocolate, contemplating about adding some booze to it; what does it matter? I can't go anywhere. Although I have to use the axe, being intoxicated wouldn't be the ultimate idea. I am relatively fond of all my digits. Speaking of this axe, I need to head outside and cut some wood. I had to watch videos on how to cut wood correctly. The company I rented the cabin from didn't bother stocking wood for me. I guess they were too busy enjoying their stress-free life. Wish I could relate.

My phone kept blowing up from the asshole ex until I lost service. I just hope her pussy was worth it. Merry fuckin Christmas to you, Noel.

I slam back my hot chocolate before heading out, warming up my insides. I take a deep breath before I struggle to tug these snow pants on. I jump, tug, and kick. I'm not going to lie. I don't look attractive right now. I'm out of breath by the time I pull my toque on. Swinging the door open, I get a blast of winter wind. Snow blows in, sending chills deep down to my bones. I took the first step in the snow, and I was already cold. I can't see for shit from the snow being whipped in my face.

I grumble as I try to walk down the stairs. I swear, if I land on my ass, just leave me to die of hypothermia. They can find my body in the spring if the animals don't eat me first. It'll be the perfect way to go. I trudge through the snow to the woodpile, wondering if they have a gun somewhere in this house. That would be better than what I'm going through. I give my head a shake. I have to get out of this funk that I'm in. Yes, I caught the ex in the shittiest way I possibly could, but come on. I'm in the mountains at Christmas time. It is beautiful when you overlook a few minor things, like the *weather.*

I grab the axe from the stump before I set a log down. I feel like a wannabe lumberjack. All I'm missing is, well, everything. I'm so out of my element.

I'm about to swing the axe when I hear a minor rev coming from the trees. That's interesting. I haven't heard a soul out here in the three days since I arrived. It could be other cabin folk braving this shit snow. I don't care, but don't bug me. I'm the Grinch this holiday season.

I swing the axe down, splitting the log. One point for Noel. Zero points for the log.

I continue cutting logs while every part of my body continues freezing. That stupid sound from the snowmobile is still in the woods, getting more and more on my nerves. I wanted some peace and quiet, hence why I chose this place. I take my tiny stack of wood back into the cabin, grumbling the entire way.

I stomp the snow off my boots before I try to kick them off. I stumble, falling on my ass. Logs fly over my head, landing with loud thumps. My ass is sore, but so is my ego. Thankfully, no one is around to see my greatest downfall. After I lie here for a bit, thinking about what my life has become and picking myself up, I kick one log towards the fireplace. Take that, you stupid piece of shit.

I'm trying to remember why I decided to come all the way out here instead of somewhere warm. I could've gone anywhere, okay, maybe not anywhere. My pocketbook isn't that deep. I was lucky enough to have this place pre-booked as a surprise gift. Good thing I never mentioned it.

Building a fire is a little easier than I thought it would be. I curl up on the couch with a blanket, listening to the wood crackle. This would be perfect if only I had someone to cuddle with me.

I must've dozed off because I woke up in a dark cabin; the fire was nothing but smouldering embers. I rub my hands on my thighs to warm them up. I try to untangle my legs from the blanket, but I only end up falling off the couch.

"Ouch," I mumble.

Why am I such a klutz? I'm honestly surprised I didn't lose a finger cutting wood.

I get up, moving to the window that overlooks the driveway. The moon is shining so brightly that I can see the snowflakes still falling. If you look upwards, it's like you're shooting into space in a rocket ship. It's truly a beautiful sight. My gaze scans the landscape, so white and magical. If I loved Christmas, this would infuse me with jolliness.

I eventually make it to the bedroom; it's not a giant room. The king bed is what you'd expect in a cabin. The frame is made from logs; the bedding is surprisingly newer, minus the fact that it's all Christmas patterned. All the colours in the world, and they choose this shit. Ugh. I'll never be able to escape it. I swear, if the sugar plum fairy comes to visit me in my dreams, I'm done. Crawling under the covers, I swish my feet around, warming up the sheets. Once it's relatively warm, my eyes drop.

A stream of light wakes me up. You know, for being someone on vacation, I'm supposed to sleep in. After finding my slippers, I head for the kitchen. I need some perk-me-up juice. Unfortunately, it's too early for alcohol, so coffee will have to do. I also have to light another fire. I tell you, roughing it is more challenging than I thought. But I still wouldn't change a thing—well, maybe one thing.

I crack open the front door and am immediately greeted with a blanket of snow. As a bonus, it has stopped snowing. I couldn't tell you the colour of my SUV because the snow is so thick. I'll have to shovel today. That'll be a great workout. I can't get lazy on vacay.

I'm halfway done with the driveway when the sound of snowmobiles approaches. It's the most annoying sound in the world. People are out here for the peace and quiet, not to hear your loud ass machines. They only grow louder the closer they get. I go back to my shovelling, ignoring the world.

Well, I ignored the world so well that I never heard anyone come near me.

A deep voice scares the shit out of me, making me swing my shovel backwards. A hand grabs my shovel right before it makes contact.

"Jesus! Trying to kill me?"

I turn around and come face-to-face with, hands down, the most gorgeous man I have ever seen. He's so pretty that I'm sure I'm drooling. His lips are also moving, and I arch an eyebrow, wondering what the hell he's talking about because all I'm thinking about is his appearance under all that winter gear. He snaps his fingers, and I blink, breaking whatever spell I am under. I pull my shovel out of his grasp.

"Were you listening to me? Did you have a stroke or something?"

I discreetly wipe my mouth with my mitts just to be safe. "Um, sorry, no. Could you repeat that?"

He gives me a sly grin. "I was asking if you were out here all alone."

"Who wants to know?" I grip my shovel tighter.

"I'm not a killer or anything." He laughs.

I step back. "That's what they all say before they slice and dice the poor, innocent girl."

"Look, my friend and I were snowmobiling and saw you were shovelling your driveway, and we thought we could help, that's all."

"No offence or anything to those muscles, but I got this."

"How do you know I have muscle under all this padding?" He pokes at all the fluff.

I shrug. "I have a hunch. Now, if you don't mind, please take your loud, annoying toys away from my cabin. I came for peace and to wallow in self-pity."

He stares at me for a very long time, so long that I grow uncomfortable. Maybe he really is a killer, and I'm the prey. Dear God. I take another step backwards. Now, where's that axe when I need it?

"I swear I'm not a killer. I'll leave you be, but if you need anything, I'm the cabin next door that way." He points to the left.

I nod, not that I'll ever go on the lookout for him. "Thanks. I'll keep that in mind when I need a cup of sugar."

He smiles and shakes his pointer finger at me. "You're funny. I like that."

I salute him and walk back to the deck without glancing back. The sound of those machines is the last thing I hear before I close the doors.

2
North

Nothing says Christmas like being in the Rocky Mountains. I love this time of year. Everything is so magical, covered in thick snow. Yes, I sound like a chick, but you have to admit that it is the best time of the year. You never know what lies in store.

I came up to Canmore for Christmas, and my buddy Everest tagged along while his girlfriend was out of town for a few days. What we didn't expect was the blizzard of the season to hit. Lucky for us, that means we get to use the snowmobiles.

"Hurry the fuck up, man. The snow finally stopped. Let's head out before it snows again," Everest nags as he tugs on his gear.

"The fuck does it look like I'm doing here, man!" I throw my helmet at him, smacking him in the stomach with it.

"Asshole, tis' the season for giving, not being a jerk, you know."

"I'm giving you one chance before I ship you back home. You're lucky I invited you on this trip."

He only rolls his eyes before he steps outside. I love this cabin more than anything. The Christmas tree is decorated in red and green. Christmas lights are strung across the wooden mantle with stockings. When the fire is burning, it reminds me of my childhood, waiting for Santa to come and fill them.

If you couldn't tell, I'm very much still into Christmas. It's another reason why I love coming up to the mountains. It's magical.

We tried riding yesterday, but it was a bust with the snow falling so heavily. With a fresh fall, we'll have to take it easy. The snowplows won't be out until later today. Lucky for us, no one will be on the roads. We're soon ripping through the trees without a care in the world when Everest signals me to head for the road.

I can see someone outside when we are near the closest neighbouring cabin. I slow down and notice they are shovelling their driveway. Now, my ma always taught me to be neighbourly, so I'm inclined to think there's nothing wrong with showing a helping hand, especially after all the snow we got overnight. I stop at the end of the driveway, letting Everest know I'll be right back. It's probably a little old lady. The last thing I need is for her to break a hip.

I clear my throat when I get closer, only to be greeted with a shovel travelling straight for my head. I grab it, stopping it just in time to avoid being smacked in the face.

"Jesus! Are ya trying to kill me? Are you out here alone?"

The old lady turns around, except it's no old lady. I'm staring at the most adorable woman I have ever seen. Her nose is the brightest red from the cold, making her green eyes stand out. The toque she's wearing has a pom pom on top. She stares at me forever.

"Are you listening to me? Did you have a stroke or something?"

I watch as she tries to wipe her mouth discreetly. It's funny if you think about it. "Um, sorry, no. Could you repeat that?"

I can't help but grin. If she only knew that I was also checking her out, but at least I learned how to do it more slyly. "I asked if you were out here all alone."

"Who wants to know?"

"I'm not a killer or anything." I laugh, glancing toward Everest.

I watch as she takes a subtle step back. "That's what they all say before they slice and dice the poor, innocent girl."

I raise a brow. "Look, my friend and I were out snowmobiling and saw you shovelling your driveway. We thought we could help, that's all."

"No offence or anything to those muscles. But I got this."

I can't help but flex my ab muscles under my coat at her compliment. "How do you know I have muscles under all this padding?" I poke at all the fluff.

Her tiny shoulders raise. "I have a hunch. Now, if you don't mind, take your loud, annoying toys away from my cabin. I came for peace and to wallow in self-pity."

I watch her momentarily, trying to get a read on her. Why is she out here all by herself? I assume she's alone because if she had a boyfriend or a husband, he would be shovelling out here. At least, he should be. She shifts as if I am making her uncomfortable—*way to go, North, you idiot.*

"I swear I'm not a killer. I'll leave you be, but if you need anything, I'm the cabin next door that way." I point in the direction from which I just came.

She gives me a quick nod. "Thanks. I'll keep that in mind when I need a cup of sugar."

I smile and shake my index finger at her. "You're funny. I like that." It's hard to find someone you can joke around with, and so far, this entire conversation has been nothing but laid back.

She gives me a salute and walks back to the deck. I head back to my snowmobile and start it up. Everest gives me a little grin, and I shoot him the middle finger before taking off. I'll come back alone later to shovel if she hasn't finished it yet. That's a big job for someone her size. I'm not saying she can't do it on her own. Don't get me wrong; I'm all for girl power and shit. Good thing my Ma can't hear my thoughts. She would surely tan my hide.

The afternoon flies by, and I am exhausted and cold when we finally reach the cabin. The thought of starting that fire looks more desirable by the second, as well as a cup of hot chocolate with a splash of booze.

"You sure were giving that little lass the eye." Everest laughs on his way into the kitchen.

I find a small snowball on the floor and chuck it at him. "You shut that fuckin' mouth. I thought she was a little old lady at first."

"Aha, sure ya did. What gave it away? The plaid snowsuit? Or the furry boots?"

I roll my eyes, walking around him. "Remind me again why I invited you out here?"

"Best friend, remember."

"Please don't. I only took pity on you because no one else wanted to play with you in the playground."

He snorts in his mug. "Is that what your Ma tells you when the dog won't play with you?"

"You're such a hoser. When are you leaving, anyway?" I get busy making my booze-filled hot cocoa.

"Depends on the plows. I told Ivy I'd be back by the twenty-third for sure. Her family wants to host a game night, so I promised to make it. What about you?"

"About that. I was thinking of staying up here for Christmas. I'm not sure yet. You know how everyone nags me about finding a girlfriend for this time of year. It gets on my nerves."

He laughs. That's because he's never been single for any holiday before. He doesn't understand the pressure. My brother and his wife are expecting their second child, and my sister is bringing her boyfriend home for the second time. That leaves the single as a pringle to be picked on. I love my family, don't get me wrong, but the pressure is too much. I don't want them to ruin my favourite holiday.

After supper, I leave Everest alone so I can go back over to the neighbour. It's been bugging me that I didn't help with her driveway or get her name. The plows came out and did somewhat of a decent job of clearing the roads. I saw how she glared at the snowmobiles, so I fired up the truck instead. I need one less reason for her to be pissed off with me.

When I reach the entrance to her driveway, I notice the massive pile of snow from the plow. There's no way in or out of her driveway. I'm glad I showed up when I did. I grab the shovel from the truck box, ready to work. The wind picks up out of nowhere, whipping the snow from the trees down on me. Well, this didn't turn out how I wanted it to. However, I hear a beautiful sound coming down the road.

"Yeah, you think it's funny being shit on by the trees?" I turn to look at my mystery girl.

"I actually do. It's what you get for trespassing."

I drop my mouth. Here I am doing something nice for her, and she has the balls, no, sorry, the lady balls, to tell me that I'm trespassing. "I'm shovelling your driveway for you, lady."

"Yep, I got that. But I can handle it."

"Wow, all right. Try to do one nice thing, and I get reprimanded," I mumble to myself. I head back to my truck.

"Wait!" she yells. "I'm sorry for being a dick. Wanna come in and warm up?"

The snow crunches under my boots when I turn to look at her. "Are you the killer in this situation now?"

She laughs, shaking her head. "Please, like I would tell you either way." She walks back to her cabin.

This is it. I either follow her or head back and miss my chance again.

3

Noel

Oh my God, oh my God. I can't believe I asked a complete stranger into my cabin. A hot stranger, I might add. I'm having a mild freakout, and now I'm struggling to get out of my coat. I managed to get the zipper stuck right at my lady parts. I keep struggling until large hands stop mine.

"Need a hand?"

I look up at a light shade of hazel eyes. "Oh, um. Nah, I got it. The coat is old, that's all." He gives me that sly grin again, making me swallow hard.

He removes his hand from mine, and I try to look like I'm not struggling still. I finally give up and slip it down my body—his deep laugh echoes in the cabin.

"I could've just helped you. That looked to be harder than it should've been."

I bite my lip and walk into the kitchen. I reminded myself that I didn't have to invite him inside, but I did, so I should be polite. "What can I get you?"

"Coffee and maybe your name."

I startle when I find him next to me. "Right, I'm Noel."

"North," he says.

"Interesting name."

"I could say the same, considering you are named after the holidays, and your cabin is lacking." He looks around with disapproval.

"Well, bah humbug." I pour him a coffee in a white coffee mug. I placed all the Christmas ones in the very back of the cupboard. If I had the choice, I would change my bed linens too.

He shakes his head at me. "Wow, I don't think I've ever met a real-life Grinch before. Tell me. How big is your heart?"

"Big enough not to care, that's for sure." I watch as he walks into the living room, shaking his head.

"I can't believe you don't have a tree or any stockings. Where is Santa going to place your coal? What are you doing out here if it's not to bask in the Christmas spirit?"

"Personal reasons." I sit in the leather chair, keeping my distance from him so I can watch him snoop in my space. He drinks as he walks around. "What are you doing up here?" I ask.

"Personal reasons." He repeats, placing his mug down on the table.

"A getaway with your boyfriend?"

"Excuse me?" he stutters.

"The boyfriend. I saw him on the other snowmobile. I take it that's why you're up here."

He sits on the couch, glaring at me. "I'm not gay. I'm as straight as they come."

I nod eagerly, going along with him. "Sure, you are."

He gets up suddenly, coming at me. He blocks me in my chair with hands on either side of me, his nose almost touching mine.

"Trust me, I love women and know how to satisfy them. The only name they yell in bed is mine."

I lick my lips, watching his gaze flicker to my lips. How the hell did we get here? I should've run with the serial killer line a little longer. I stare into his eyes. One small move and our lips will touch. I'll be honest. I do wonder what they will feel like. I tilt my head slightly.

"Prove it," I whisper.

That fuckin' grin again. His lips lower on mine, slowly capturing my bottom lip in between his. He cups my cheek, and as he sucks on my lip, I moan the neediest moan of my life. I grip the front of his shirt, pulling him closer. My panties are soaking wet from a kiss. He guides his hand into my hair and holy hell, it feels like heaven. My ex never did this before; his kisses were sloppy like a dog's. When I kiss North, it's completely different. Maybe it's because I barely know him.

When he pulls away, his eyes are filled with lust.

"This is crazy, right? I don't think I've ever felt something this strong for someone this fast before," he says, still holding onto my head.

"I don't know. It is crazy. Maybe it's the weather."

"Could be." He kisses me again before backing away. "When did you come up here?" He sits back down, grabbing his mug as if nothing happened. At the same time, I'm trying to wonder how to form words.

I sip on my coffee instead, watching him. He's wearing a tight black Henley and dark wash jeans, and his hair is a mess from being tucked under his hat. I feel like a perv just watching him.

"I've been here for two days already or something like that. I don't know. I lost track of time."

"Almost the same time as Everest and me then. He's headed home tomorrow, I think. His girlfriend's family has a bunch of Christmas things planned."

I pull my feet under me, getting cozy. "That's nice. What about you? Headed back for Christmas?"

He gets up, adds another log to the fire and stands there watching the flames. "I'm not sure. There's so much pressure from my siblings to bring home their significant others. I don't want to hear it anymore."

"Can't relate to that, sorry."

He tilts his head, turning those hazel eyes to me. "Your family isn't big on Christmas, are they?"

"It's only been my dad and me since my mom passed away. He stopped celebrating Christmas. It was her favourite holiday. He didn't want any reminders of happiness in the house. So, with every passing year, this month becomes shittier and shittier for me. I'm beginning to think I'm cursed."

He moves over, dropping to his knees in front of me. He caresses my leg while peering into my eyes. "I'm so sorry, Noel," he whispers gently.

I give him a tight smile. "I try not to think about it too much, but he could've tried harder, at least for her. Sorry, I didn't mean to spill my darkest shit on you. We don't even know each other."

He shrugs, still caressing my leg. "I have that effect on people. My Ma says it's because I'm the youngest, but who knows." Then he smacks me on the leg. "I have an idea. You need some Christmas cheer, and I need a Christmas date."

"Do I? I enjoy being the Grinch, to be honest." I arch a brow at him.

He grunts. "Listen, I'm not joking. My family will eat me alive if I don't show up with someone. Please, I'm begging you with gingerbread cookies. Do me this favour, and I'll help break your Christmas curse."

I drop my head into my hands. "I don't know. I hardly know you."

"That's fair. Then will you go on a date with me tomorrow? It'll be step one of making you a little less Scroogie."

I narrow my eyes. "I am not a Scrooge. I still donate to the Salvation Army."

"Soooo?"

"Yes, I'll go on a date with you, Mr. Annoying."

He stands up, kissing me once more and leaning more into it. "I'll see you first thing, Miss. Grinch."

I watch as he dresses and leaves the cabin. That man knows how to kiss. That's all I know, and tomorrow I'm going to find out what he can do for a date. I can't believe I'm going along with this. What the hell did I just sign up for?

Fake dating for the holidays is a new low, even for me.

4
North

The drive back to the cabin is quicker than I want it to be. I barely have time to wrap my head around what I just asked Noel to do. Be my fake date for Christmas. Am I crazy? It has to be the weather or the time of year. My family is driving me so crazy that I'm desperate enough to find some random girl to pretend to be my girlfriend. Oh God, it's going to be a gong show.

Everest is packing when I step inside. "You leaving me finally?"

"Yeah, I told Ivy the roads are open, so she wants me home tonight. Sorry, bro."

I wave him off. "That's fine. I actually made plans with the neighbour next door."

"Really? Do I wanna know?"

I run my hand through my hair. "I, um, sorta asked her to be my date for Christmas dinner."

He drops his clothes in his bag; he opens and closes his mouth and rubs his forehead. "Are you serious? What the fuck were you thinking?"

I plop myself into the armchair, hanging my legs over the side. "Clearly, I wasn't. We were just talking, and the next minute, I was kissing her. My mind was a switchboard. Her place is anti-Christmas, so in exchange, I told her I would help her find her Christmas joy if she sorta helped me."

"Wow," he breathes.

"Yep," I sigh, popping the P.

I watch as he walks through the cabin grabbing all his shit, as I contemplate my life. I think I'm doing the right thing. She could use a little comfort and joy. Two birds, one stone kinda thing. I got this. I'll deal with Ma after the fact.

"All right, man, I'm out. Good luck with...What is her name?"

"Noel, something or rather. We didn't exchange last names."

He bursts out in laughter. "Wait until she finds out who you are."

My shoulders sink forward. “That’s what I’m afraid of. I’m gonna hold out for as long as I can. Safe travels. Say hi to Ivy for me.”

I didn’t even think about Noel finding out who I am. Maybe she won’t figure it out. I’m not usually in the public eye, so I’m not well known. It’s only my name. Thinking about Noel reminds me of our date tomorrow. I need to think of a few ideas to get her into the spirit.

I wake up more excited and nervous than I should be. What if she hates my ideas? I didn’t even ask her what she likes; I’m only going off what Google says are the most romantic dates to do around Christmas. When has the internet ever lied? I make two to-go mugs of hot chocolate, tossing in some mini marshmallows and head for her cabin.

When she opens the door, I’m blown away. Her honey-blonde hair is braided, framing each side of her face. She's one of the few I’ve noticed who doesn’t need to wear a ton of makeup and still looks gorgeous. Luckily for her, I grew up with a sister, so I know a thing or two.

“Hello, North. How are you today?” She moves back, letting me inside.

"Better now that I'm here. Are you excited for today?" I grab her coat off the coat rack, opening it for her.

She steps into it. "Are you always this excited? Because, no offence, it's disgusting. Take it down a notch."

"No can do. Christmas joy, remember? Come on, and I have a gift for you in the truck."

She grumbles something under her breath as she tugs on her boots. I stifle a laugh but reach for and kiss her when she comes up. "Couldn't help myself. I enjoy kissing these lips."

"If it makes you feel better, I enjoy kissing yours, too," she utters.

I take her hand while walking to the truck. When we reach the truck, I open the door for her, maybe checking out her ass as she climbs into the cab. The first chance I get, I'm smacking that. My hand tingles just thinking about it.

"So, Noel, where do you live?" I turn onto the main road, heading into Canmore, the town located down the mountain.

"I live in Calgary, so being out here is completely out of the norm for me."

I glance over, and she's taking in the sights. My family has been coming out here for as long as I can remember, not just in the winter. We own the cabin resort. It makes it perfect to have a getaway whenever any of us feel like it.

“I’m sure by the time you leave. The city will feel weird. Here, I made you hot cocoa.” I pass her a cup, and she breaks into a stunning smile.

“Thanks.” She takes a sip, and her eyes widen. “And you added marshmallows! Tell me something about yourself; where did you grow up?”

“I grew up here, surprisingly.”

“Oh, wow, that must've been nice.” She sips her drink again.

“It was. My sister and brother are only a year apart, but me? I decided to be a late bloomer and come into the world six years after my parents thought they were finished. We eventually moved, but we come here every year.”

“Is this where they are now? Or what? I guess I should be asking questions as the fake girlfriend.”

“They are. Ma and Pops moved back after retirement. I think their hearts never left this town.” It’s a laidback town to love, that’s for sure. Almost everyone knows everyone. Sometimes that sucks, especially when you are trying to lie low. Heading into town is probably my stupidest idea, but I’m sure it’ll be worth it. “Have you been into town yet?”

“Um, only to drive to the cabin. Then it snowed. Poor planning on my part, so I’m thankful that you came along.”

"I'll tell you this right now. It's a tiny town. Very centred on Christmas."

"Great," she grumbles.

I pat her thigh. "You'll do perfectly. It's my job to make you happy. You never did tell me why you came up here."

She exhales loudly. "It's personal."

"Mmhmm, but if you're going to be my girlfriend, we probably should know a thing or two about each other."

She leans her head back on the headrest, tilting a little to look at me. "Ever been with someone that you thought was the one?" I shake my head. "I have. We had been together for three years, practically living with each other, when I came home from work one night earlier than expected. I walked in on him fucking my best friend."

I reach out for her hand, stroking my thumb on the back of it. "He's a piece of shit, Noel. Men like that don't know what they have until it's gone."

"Yeah, well, I slashed their tires, so fuck them. Right?" She grins.

"That's right. See, I knew you might be that serial killer after all." I slowly release my hand, only for her to tighten her grip.

I pulled the truck into the parking lot of our first-date destination. "All right, are you ready for this?"

She looks out through the front window. "What is this place?"

"It's the hockey arena. Come on, let's get this show on the road." I exit the cab, grabbing my hockey bag from the box before moving to her side and helping her down.

"I haven't gone skating since I was a kid."

I wrap my arm around her shoulder, guiding her to the building. I can't wait for this.

5

Noel

Skating. I'm skating.

I'm like a newborn calf standing for the first time because my legs do not want to cooperate with my brain. Maybe I should've told him I'm a klutz. Oh, I'm gonna cut a finger off for sure. I'm hanging onto the rink boards, refusing to let go. All the while, North laughs at me.

"Come on, Noel. It's not that bad. I'll hold your hand." He holds it out. "The entire time."

"Promise?" I go to look at him more, and my legs go out in either direction. I grip the edge of the board tighter. "North, this is the worst thing ever." His hands go around my waist to help me up.

"I got you, I promise," he whispers in my ear. His breath stirs my hair, sending chills down my spine.

I dig my fingers into his forearm as my skates glide across the ice. I wobble slightly, but he never lets me go. "How are you so good at this?" my voice hitches as I lose my balance again.

"I played hockey as a kid and into my teenage years."

"Of course you did. Still, do I gather?"

"Only for fun. A few friends will get together when we have the chance. I always hated the early mornings and the pressure of playing on a team. What about you?"

"Sports were too expensive. I think my first pair of skates came from a thrift shop, and the only reason I got them was that we were going skating for school." I smile, remembering my mom taking me. She was so excited to be buying me my first pair. They weren't freshly white like all the other girls in my class, and I didn't have a fancy bag to carry them in, but she was determined to buy them. She said there wasn't a chance that her little girl was missing out on her first time skating. She passed away a year later, and I haven't touched a pair of skates since.

North stops us, swiping away a tear I didn't know had fallen. "You doing all right?"

I clear my throat from the tightness. "Yep, sorry, just thinking of my mom. Stupid Christmas."

He pulls me into his chest, and I inhale his cologne deeply. "I should've asked about skating first. I'm failing at this fake boyfriend thing already."

"I don't think so. Just a minor setback, maybe?" I try to shrug, but I end up falling, taking North with me. He twists me so I land on his chest. I land with an oomph. "Fuck, I should also tell you I'm a klutz."

He rubs the back of his head. "I see that. So, bubble wrap the next time we try this? Gotcha."

I smack him on the chest. "Shut it. It's not my fault."

"Come on. I have something else in mind that should be safer."

He gets up so smoothly that I sit on my ass and can only watch as I think of crawling to the opening in the wall. I'm about to do just that when he picks me up.

I squeal, clinging to his neck. "Put me down before I break a leg or, worse, kill you."

"Have a little faith. Remember, I'm a pro on the skates, baby." He gives me that sly grin again.

I'm beginning to hate that grin. It only spells out trouble.

What I wasn't expecting for stop two was an outdoor market.

"North, I think you don't like me." I'm staring at all the red and green in horror.

He chuckles in that deep voice. "That's where you're wrong. We only have one day until Christmas, so dig deep, my dear. I know you have some cheer left somewhere."

He's all but smiles when he's looking at all the shoppers. He intertwines our fingers, tugging me like a puppy; I feel like one who wants to lie down and play dead.

"I hate you so much right now."

"I'll change your mind. Besides, how can you hate me? I shovelled your driveway. That has to count for something." He pulls my toque down past my eyes before walking away.

"Eh, you asshole." I run after him, catching up to him at an ornament booth. "You have too long legs. It's not fair."

"Not my fault, small fry. What do you think of this one?" He holds up an ornament with a tiny cabin inside and a snowy landscape. I've never seen such a thing before. He holds it with such care that I remember when those hands were holding me.

"I think this would be perfect for my ma. What do you think?" He's still looking at the ornament and smiling. It must mean something to him if he wants to buy it.

"I think she would love it, especially if it's coming from you."

He hands it back to the lady as we watch her wrap it in a festive wrap. "One down, four more to go. I guess I should get my sister's boyfriend something, right?"

"I mean, probably. Do you know him?" I grab the gift bag as he pays for it.

"Not well. He's some douche from the city who wears loafers." He rolls his eyes. "I can't even remember his name, Brian, Bran, something like that."

"You know, what about liquor? Can't go wrong with a bottle of whiskey or rum." I point in the direction of a liquor booth.

I watch his eyes light up. "Genius! I can grab my Pops something while we're there." He kisses the top of my head before taking off.

It's like watching a kid in a candy store. I'm not lying when I say North is the polar opposite of any guy I would ever date. He's like a breath of fresh air. Maybe it's the mountain air that's changing me. There's just something about him, though, that I can't quite place my finger on. He's so down to earth, and well, I'm the most stressed-out person around. I'm already stressing about meeting his family. What if I blow it for him? He's counting on me to be his girlfriend. I don't have to worry about faking the chemistry. We have plenty. I can't deny that. What I lack is well, grace and cheer. I don't want to ruin his favourite time of the year, so if I don't feel jolly, then what? As I watch him chat up the sales clerk, talking about which bottle of whiskey he should buy his sister's boyfriend, I wonder if I should buy his parents a gift. I can't show up empty-handed. I leave them be and wander over to a table that sells woodwork. I glance around until my eyes fall on something beautiful.

"What did you buy?" North rests his chin on my shoulder, peeking into the bag.

I close it quickly. "Something, but I can't tell you."

He turns into my neck. "A mystery, I like it." He kisses upwards to my chin. My pussy throbs for attention, and she isn't the only one. I so badly want to turn and feel those lips on mine again. "What's the matter? You look a little flushed."

"It's from all these layers." I press my cold hand to my cheek, cooling it off.

"Yeah, so if I moved my hands down here, what would happen?"

He moves his hands under my jacket, skimming across my stomach when his finger dips below my waistband. I grip his wrist.

"We are in public, and there are a lot of people."

"Scared? You might like it." He wiggles his brows.

"Let's go. You still have shopping to do."

He drapes his arm around my shoulder once again, steering me in the direction he wants to go. I'll admit his words have me twisted up inside. I hadn't done anything adventurous in the bedroom before unless you counted watching some porn when I was horny because my ex wouldn't sleep with me. Now I'm wondering if he was sleeping with my ex-best friend simultaneously. The thought of it makes me sick.

We wandered around the market until closing time. I'm still impressed with the number of people coming out in winter to shop. I'll admit it's nice that they support local shops and not the commercials that constantly push Christmas down your throat. Like, why do they have to start at the beginning of November? Give me a break!

I'll admit this is one of the best dates I've ever been on. There is zero pressure. I don't expect anything from him; I can still be me. It's okay that I fall down. North doesn't get upset or embarrassed with me or degrade me in front of everyone. Trust me. I've fallen plenty already. He does remind me about the bubble wrap occasionally.

"I had so much fun today, North. Thank you so much."

"I'm glad, but we need to work on your walking skills."

I can't help but laugh. "You know, I've been learning for nearly twenty-six years, and it isn't going as planned, so good luck."

"We can always work on the horizontal tango."

And now my panties are soaking wet.

6
North

I haven't met anyone like Noel before, and I've dated a shit ton. Maybe not telling her who I am is working, although she doesn't feel like someone who is into material things. Shopping today was something I usually dread, but somehow, being with her made it more enjoyable.

I glance over at her and notice she is passed out. I guess I wore her out. Pulling into her driveway, I place the truck in park. I watch her sleep like a mother fucking creep. Jesus Murphy, what is wrong with me? I give my head a shake before quickly stepping out. I walk to her side, opening her door.

"Noel, hey, we're home," I whisper quietly, shaking her. Her head rolls to face me.

"No, I wanna sleep," she says, her eyes still shut.

I reach over her, unbuckling the seat belt. I lift her out of the truck, bridal style, heading to the cabin. She buries her nose deeper into my neck. The warmth from her lips sends chills throughout my body. I almost drop her when she kisses my neck.

"I need you right now," I growl, pulling her closer to me.

"Please, North."

That's all I need to hear. I move her upright, wrapping her legs around me. I push her into the door, pressing my hard cock into her needy pussy, only to be greeted by a moan.

"Do you feel how much I need you?" I move my lips to her jaw, pressing small kisses along the way until I reach her lips. "Tell me what you want," I whisper against her lips.

When she speaks, her lips touch mine. "I want whatever you can give me. I want you to unwrap me like a goddamn Christmas present, North."

I can't help but groan. "I want to fuck you until you forget your name, Noel. I want to feel that sweet little pussy of yours clenching around my cock. Now, what do you want?" I kick the door open before I fuck her in the snowbank.

"North, please. I can't wait much longer." Her voice was barely a whisper. I set her down as we both strip out of our coats. I never take my eyes off her; she's my prey, and I must feast.

We barely have our boots off when I tell her. "Get your ass on that couch now."

I watch as goosebumps spring across her skin. She backs away, watching me as I undo my belt. I slide it out of my loops with a snap. I stalk over to her, giving her the sly grin I know she secretly loves.

"Hands now," I demand. She gives me her hands, crossing them over each other. I loop my belt over them, giving them a good tug. "Comfy?"

"Very."

"Good, now lie down because I'm hungry." I wait until she's fully reclined before I undo her jeans and slide them down her sweet little body. I sit between her legs, running my hands along her thighs. I watch as she squirms; her breathing hitches when my finger grazes her clit through her panties. I press my finger in firmer, and she moans, kicking her hips upwards. "I love the sounds you make, baby. But I think we can do much better, don't you?"

I move her panties to the side, staring down at her glistening wet pussy. My mouth waters when I think of all the ways I'm going to feast. I lower my face gazing up at her, meeting her eyes as I lick her clit. Her hips flex, bringing her clit closer to my face. I bury my face deeper as her fingers dig into my hair. I lift my head, taking her hands in mine.

"Keep these to yourself, or I'll make better use of them, but the fun ends down—" I tap her pussy. "Here, do you understand?"

She shifts, flexing her fingers like she's thinking about it. "Fine," she whines.

"Good girl. Now, where was I?" I move my head back down to her clit, sucking and licking. I dip a finger inside her dripping core. She cries out, but not once does she move her hands. "Fuck, baby, you feel amazing." I move my hand under her shirt, squeezing her breast.

"North, please. I need to feel you inside of me."

"I am inside of you, baby," I add another finger, curling up, hitting her g-spot. What I wasn't expecting was a wet surprise. "Mmm, baby, did you just squirt on me?"

She bites her lip. "Sorry, I should've warned you I'm a squirter. It only happens sometimes." Her cheeks turn a bright crimson.

"There's nothing to be embarrassed about. That's the hottest thing I've fuckin' seen. Now I'm going to make it my goal every time." I crawl up, pressing my lips to hers. "How do you taste? I'll let you know. You taste so fucking good." I devour her lips some more, pressing my hips into hers. My cock is about to explode if I don't get inside of her. I move my hand in between us, undoing my pants. I sit up, grabbing her hands. I undo the belt, freeing her.

"You have a condom, right?"

"Why don't you want to get pregnant from a fake boyfriend?" I reach around for my wallet.

"I don't, actually, but I really want to fuck you, so can you hurry up?"

I smile at her as I slip on the condom. "If that's what you wish for." I stroke my cock through her wetness before sinking deep. We both groan together. I grip her hips and slam into her. "God, you feel so good. Your pussy is squeezing me. I could spend all day between your legs."

"Oh, fuck. I love it when you talk like that," she moans louder—digging her nails into my back.

"Come for me, baby. Come around, my cock."

Her muscles clench around me, and I fuck her deeper, bringing her orgasm to the very edge before I flick her clit, making her scream. I can feel my orgasm coming. With my balls tightening, I go still, spilling inside the condom. I would've painted it all over her stomach if I had it my way.

We're both out of breath. I slip out of her and head to the bathroom to clean up. Leaving my jeans and shirt in the bathroom, I walk back in my boxers. I find her almost asleep on the couch.

"Come on, baby. Bedtime."

I pick her up and carry her to the bedroom. I let out a chuckle when I see the bedspread.

"Shut the hell up. It came with the cabin, and I want to puke every time I see it," she grumbles in my chest.

I set her down right on top of a Christmas tree. "I can tell it kills you just by the look on your face. I'm rather surprised you haven't exchanged it yet."

She rolls her eyes. "Trust me, I want to, but there isn't any other option." She pulls her shirt off, removing her bra, before climbing under the covers naked.

I tuck her closer, breathing in her shampoo. Tomorrow is Christmas Eve, and she still hasn't opened up to the thought of Christmas. I have my work cut out for me. I'll have to think outside of the box. I also have to inform Ma about a date I'm bringing home. Noel's gentle breathing lets me know she has already passed out. I guess skating and shopping did her in.

I only hope we can pull this off without anyone catching on that it's fake. I think we can, and I hope I didn't fuck it up by sleeping with her. We get along excellent, and we definitely know how to make each other laugh.

Here's to hoping.

7

Noel

My body is too hot. I don't recall logging on or adding an extra blanket to the bed during the night. That's when I feel something hard poking me in the back. That something isn't tiny or fuckin' average. My vag is still sore from being fucked like that. The ex was always such a bore in the bedroom. I always had to bring a toy just to guarantee I got off; he was a two-pump chump. North, on the other hand, takes the time to do foreplay. The first time my ex made me squirt, he got pissed off. He was grossed out, and he never touched me again.

I thought for sure that North would say something rude. I guess I should've known better. North brings out a different side of me, one that I didn't even know existed.

And that side is a horny little devil. I push my ass into his hard-on.

"Mmm, you keep that up, and I'll fuck that pretty little ass of yours." His voice is extra deep from sleep, making my pussy clench with need.

His fingers move along my stomach, dipping lower. He walks them down to my clit, pressing them hard and holding them there. His lips find their way to my neck.

"I would say this is the best way to wake up in the morning."

"Yeah." I breathe heavily when he finally moves his fingers in circles.

His other hand moves my leg over his hip, so he can move his cock between my ass, stroking it and feeling the wetness from my pussy.

"I want you so badly," he groans.

"What's stopping you?"

He drops his head to my shoulder. "Condom. I don't have another one."

I reach between my legs, feeling his velvety tip. I press my fingers over him, shifting my hips so he's rubbing his cock on my clit.

"Fuck me like this."

He growls, flipping me onto my back and grabbing me by my throat. He presses his hips into mine, his cock rubbing my clit.

"Is this what you wanted? Do you like when I fuck you like this? Do you want my cum all over your pretty little pussy?"

"Yes," I struggle to say.

My stomach cramps before tingles shoot to my clit. I grip the sheet tightly. I flex my hips into North more, curling my toes.

"Fuck, North. Yes, don't stop, please." I moan as I come.

He sits up, removing his hand to rub my clit and stroke himself. With a groan, he shoots his cum all over my pussy and stomach.

"Look at the mess we made." He draws little swirls in his cum before bringing his finger to my lips. "Clean it up."

I open for him, sucking his finger clean. He gives me that sly grin of his. My body is still on fire, and the way he's looking at me isn't helping. His dark hair falls in his eyes, and I can't help but brush it aside. His hazel eyes were still laced with sleep.

"Come on, let's have a shower, and I'll make us some breakfast. Then you can fill me in on what you have planned for the day."

He kisses me before pushing off the bed. "Sounds perfect to me. I've been thinking a lot, and since you passed out on me last night, you'll have to get in the spirit today. Tomorrow, you meet the family, remember?"

How can I forget? We have a lot of work cut out for us, that's for sure.

I'm busy making pancakes while North chops some logs for me. It's a great pay off, I think; I don't have to count my fingers after every swing. I'm flipping the last pancake when North comes in with an arm full of logs.

"I'm finished. How are you making out?"

I'm too busy staring at him to watch what I'm doing. I mindlessly search for my flipper and accidentally touch the griddle with my hand. The sizzle of my hand burning pulls my attention away so fast.

"Oh, fuck." I snatch my hand away, rushing for the sink. The cold water turns on before I can do it.

"Shit, Noel. Are you okay?" He gently holds my hand under the water.

I rest my head on his shoulder, my hand throbbing. "It's fine. Not the first burn I sustained. Doubt it'll be the last. Breakfast is ready."

Luckily, I didn't burn myself too severely. As I said, I've had worse. North still looks at me with concern or that I might fall and break my neck. For someone who's only known me for two days, it's nice that he's so worried.

It's also very concerning how quickly we move this fake dating. Usually, you don't sleep with someone that you are fake dating. Am I correct? I have no idea what he has planned for today, but all I know is it'll be Christmas shit everywhere. I honestly don't know if I can take much more of it before I want to curl up in a ball somewhere. So much of it reminds me of my mom. Maybe vacationing somewhere warm would've been the best idea.

I smile when North looks up at me.

"You okay?"

I nod. "Why wouldn't I be?"

"I don't know. You look a little." He tilts his head, getting a better look. "Sad, maybe. It's hard to explain. I don't want to upset you."

I reach across the table for his hand. "You're not, I promise. If you were, I would let you know in a heart-beat."

He narrows his eyes, and then, with a curt nod, he gets up. "All right, I have a ton of things planned for today. We also have to finish Christmas shopping."

"Ah yes, like every man across this great country today, they are doing the mad dash to get the last-minute shop-ping done."

"That's right, and we must beat them all to the good gifts. So, chop, chop." He claps his hands twice.

I groan when I get out of my seat. I'm going to have major regrets about this. I can already tell. That evil smirk he's sporting doesn't help, either.

8
North

Something is wrong, but she won't tell me. Ever since breakfast, she placed an emotional wall up, and I haven't been able to break it down. Am I being too pushy with all this? I'm sure she would tell me, or I would hope so. I decided to start with shopping, and I do need to finish it today. I also want to find her something small. I would feel like a dick if everyone had something to open except her. I think that would push her into the deep, dark depths of hating Christmas forever when we part at the end of this.

I wasn't kidding when I told her about the bubble wrap. It would make a funny gift, a perfect inside joke she would remember every time she looked at bubble wrap.

"I need to swing by my cabin to grab a change of clothes before we head back into town."

"Right, that probably would be a good idea."

I watch as she grabs a black peacoat this time, dressing more for shopping than for skating. She pulls her hair out of the collar, and I watch the waves tumble down her back. Then she turns those moss-green eyes on me. She gives me a small smile that doesn't reach her eyes, and it's my goal to change that.

"Come on, let me show you my cabin."

"That sounds dirty."

I can't help but laugh. "I could make it dirty if you want."

"Let's go before you get any other ideas, mister." She opens the door, letting in a gust of cold air. She wraps her arms around her stomach. "Why does it always have to be so cold around this time of year?"

"That's because Santa can't fly unless it's cold, silly." I guide her outside, closing the door behind me.

"Don't start with that shit; that jolly ass can't control the weather."

I open the truck door for her, helping her inside. "Are you sure you're okay?" I brush a stray strand of hair out of her face. She stops my hand.

"I said I was fine. Trust me."

I close my eyes, exhaling slowly. "All right. Please tell me when you're ready." Closing the door, I move to the driver's side. All I can do is wait until she's ready to talk.

The cabin is only a few clicks down the road. I probably should've cleaned it before I left. It's still messy from when Everest was packing. Turning into the driveway, I hear Noel whisper a *wow.* It is a little extreme for a cabin; my parents didn't cheap out when they remodelled it. The cabin is a large timber frame house. It's large enough for a family of seven. My ma wanted nothing but windows overlooking those mountains. So, my pops delivered.

"Did you want to come in?" I ask after I park the truck.

"Um, there's nothing that I can break, is there? It's so much fancier than my cabin."

"Don't be silly. It's just another place."

"Right." She opens her door without waiting for me.

I meet her at the front door, and with a deep breath, I open it. I guide her in, praying she doesn't care about a man being messy.

"Make yourself at home. I'll be right back." I quickly race up the stairs to my room. I don't think I've ever kicked off my pants this fast, even when I was a teenager, ready for my first night with a girl. If that doesn't tell you how nervous I am about her being alone, then I don't know you.

I tug on a fresh pair of jeans and a black Henley top with a plaid button up. I brush my teeth and throw on some cologne and deodorant before taking the stairs, two by two. I find her gawking at the Christmas tree.

"I almost forgot that your place would look like a full-blown Hallmark movie."

"I did warn you it is my favourite holiday, remember?" I walk up behind her, wrapping my arms around her midsection and resting my chin on her shoulder.

"How could I forget?" I watch as she reaches for an ornament. It's a handmade one. I think my brother made it. I reach for it before she turns it around and finds his name.

"Let's go, Grinch. The world awaits us."

She elbows me in the stomach. "That's not funny."

"Calling it how it is, Miss. Lump of Coal."

"Oh, my God. Stop." She turns in my arms and glares at me. "You're not funny."

I smile down at her. "I am a little funny; admit it."

She rolls her eyes. "Let's go before it's too late to shop, and besides, this isn't getting me very jolly."

I let her go, an epic fail, but I can get her back. If I can't make her happy, my family can. I guarantee that.

I slip my boots on and grab my jean jacket. Out of the corner of my eye, I notice that she's scanning my body. I turn to meet her gaze. My heart races when she moves towards me. She grabs the front flaps of my jacket, pulling me forward.

"It's unfair that you can look this good, and I look like a homeless person." She runs her hands down her black coat, the one I want to tear the fuck off so I can bend her over the couch right now.

"Not a fat chance. You are anything but. I had to dress like this so I didn't look like your servant boy."

"Now you look like my farm boy." She winks at me.

I grab her hand. "We wasted enough time, and I need you to help me shop. I also have a few dates to take you out on. Ready?"

With a curt nod. "Ready, partner."

"Now, who's being an ass."

The weather changes halfway to town. I should've checked the weather before leaving. If we get another massive dump of snow, we won't be going anywhere for a long time, and neither of us is dressed for a breakdown. I don't want to take her to Ma's tonight, but we might have to if this shit doesn't go away. She keeps staring out the window, chewing her bottom lip.

"Doing all right over there?"

"Mmm-hmm. I wasn't expecting snow, but we should've known better. After all, we are in the mountains in December."

"Don't worry. I'm an expert at driving in snow."

She glances over at me. "Yeah? You do it a lot for work or something?"

Right. Work. I guess we never talked about what we do for a living, and I don't want to talk about that. "You could say that I have meetings and drive a shit ton. What about you? What do you do for work?"

"Nothing that exciting, unfortunately. I work as the accountant clerk for an oilfield company in the city." She shrugs.

"Not your dream job, I take it."

"Fuck no, but it pays the bills. So I can't complain too much. You can't pay your bills on hopes and dreams now, right? Is your job your dream job?"

Do I want to be the ultimate douche or be honest for once? "It is. I love my job."

She inclines her head sideways and presses her lips together in a nod. "That's great, North. I'm glad you found something you love and look forward to every single day."

She goes back to staring out the window, watching the snowfall. Maybe what her life is missing is joy and not only the Christmas spirit.

9

Noel

I can't get out of this funk that I landed in, and North is trying everything he can to get me out. I only wish I could. I don't mean to be the Debbie Downer of this two-person show of ours. I think I need to get away from him for a few hours or call my dad. Does that make me a horrible person? He looks so excited to be out here shopping for his nephew. I don't want to burst that bubble of his. Just because I can't get into the spirit doesn't mean I have to bring someone else down with me. I learned that years ago. Too bad my dad never picked up on that.

"Hey, what about this? Do you think he'll love it?" North holds up some sort of toy car.

I give him a thumbs up. Cause, honestly, what do I know about kids? He gives me a look, one that I would rather not have. The look that says are you okay? He's been doing that all morning. All I can do is smile in return because what else is there to do? I move around the busy toy shop, looking at all the weird toys. I don't recall having such things when I was little. How times have changed.

I finally can't take it and move outside. The sidewalk is just as busy. The snow has lightened up a little, leaving a minor scuff across the road. I walk up the sidewalk to a bench, deciding this will be my chance to call my dad.

With a deep breath, I hit the dial button. The phone rings once, twice, and on the third ring, a voice answers, making me miss home.

"Well, hello, dearest daughter."

I smile a little at his greeting, which he always uses on me. "Hello, Dad. I'm not bugging you, am I?"

I'm sure I can hear a hockey game playing in the background, one that he recorded days ago. I'm also sure he's watched it already.

"Nah, just watching the highlights of the last game. You know how it is with these guys. They can never get their act together when the holidays are near."

"Don't I know it." Honestly, I don't. I stopped watching hockey when my papa died, and he can't figure out why I won't watch it with him. It was our thing.

"What's wrong, snow cone?"

I also hate that stupid nickname. "Nothing," I speak with my head bowed.

"I miss her too. It's okay to be still sad. You have to remember all the good times you had with her, and maybe it was wrong of me not to celebrate Christmas after she died; it wasn't fair to you." His voice hitches, but he's a strong man and would never cry.

"It's not your fault. She was your love, Dad. It's hard seeing her name everywhere I look." Even now, if I glance down the street, I'll see the word Joy at least five times in a row—a tear trickles down my nose.

Growing up, it was always Joy and Noel. We were a team, and now it's just Noel. Don't get me wrong. I have my dad, but Laurance and Noel don't have the same ring.

"How're the mountains treating you? You could come home anytime, you know." Always the perfect man for changing the subject.

"The mountains are great." This would be the perfect time to tell him about North, but something stops me.

"I feel a but coming snow cone. What is it?"

I can already tell North is watching me from up the street; turning my head, my eyes land on his. His eyebrows furrow before he walks closer to me.

"It's nothing, Dad. Can I call you later?"

"Of course, I love you."

"Love you too." I hang up right when North reaches me.

His hand cups my face, tilting it upwards. His thumb swipes my tears away. He gently shakes his head. "This was a horrible idea, wasn't it? I'm the worst person ever. We can head back to the cabin if you want to."

I place my hand over his. "What about your shopping? I honestly can't be the Grinch in front of your family."

He holds up two bags, shaking them. "I'm finished. Do you need anything?"

I probably should get him something, but what could I get him that doesn't scream *I've only known you for three days.* I need to be out here, if not for me, at least for Mom. She would love to be here shopping and enjoying all the Christmas spirit.

"Actually, can we spend more time down here?"

He smiles. "Anything you want, baby." He grabs my hand as we walk down the sidewalk.

We stop at a small café for something to eat. I found Dad a small present even though we hadn't exchanged gifts in years. I think he'll love this one, and hopefully, it'll help him move forward too. As we wait in line, I notice North eyeing one of the travel mugs. I still haven't found something for him. It's been hard when he won't leave me alone. After ordering, we find an empty table, which surprises us both, considering how busy it is here.

"What else do you have planned for us?"

He finishes chewing. "I can't say. I rather like giving you surprises." He grins that sly grin of his.

"Are you always so optimistic and cheery?"

"As the youngest, I needed to be. And to be honest, I had the shittest time in school. I was the weird, awkward kid who kept to himself. I never talked to anyone. So, a lot of kids bullied me for that. It wasn't until high school that Everest literally stumbled into me and never left. I don't know what I would have done if he had never found me when he did. I was at the lowest point of my life."

I watch him roll his sleeve up, showing me his tattoo. I noticed it this morning but didn't find it in my place to ask. I always hate when people ask about other people's tattoos. If they wanted to talk about them, they would.

"I got this when I turned eighteen." He runs his finger along the mountain and tree tattoo on his forearm. "Everest and I have the same tattoo."

"It's beautiful, North."

His lips smile faintly. "Thanks. You always have to remember where your journey starts. Then, no matter what, you can conquer anything."

I can feel my heart grow a little larger, not for the fact that it's Christmas. It's because of this man alone. I'm still having a hard time believing it's only been three days since we've known each other. How is this possible? Pinch me, please.

"Finish up. I have to use the little boys' room."

I almost spit my coffee out. "The little boys' room?"

"What? Want me to say I have to take a leak in front of the little old ladies?"

I wave him away, laughing when I look at the table filled with little old ladies. They are glaring at North's back. I wait until I see him walk into the washroom before I rush to the front counter, grabbing the travel mug. I pay, and I'm back in my seat before he walks out. He hasn't a clue that I just bought him a gift.

I'm nailing this Christmas shopping thing.

10
North

I knew something was upsetting Noel when I was in the toy store. I watched her leave the shop and walk along the sidewalk until she disappeared from my sight. I wanted to follow, but I could tell she needed to be alone. Growing up with a sister, I learned to read the signs.

I didn't expect to find her crying on a goddamn park bench, crying over seeing her mom's name everywhere during the holiday season. When she looked up at me, I lost it as I saw the tears rolling down her face.

I cup her face, tilting it upwards, watching her eyes. With a thumb, I swipe away her tears. I feel like a complete dick bag. I gently shake my head with so much regret for bringing her out here. "This was a horrible idea, wasn't it? I'm the worst person ever. We can head back to the cabin if you want to."

She places her cold hand over mine. "What about your shopping? I honestly can't be the Grinch in front of your family."

I hold up two bags, shaking them. "I'm finished. Do you need anything?" I found exactly what I needed for my nephew and sister. Everyone is finished. Now, all my focus will be on her.

"Actually, can we spend more time down here?"

That's all I need to hear, so I give her a small smile. "Anything you want, baby." I grab her hand, help her up, and walk down the sidewalk. I have a few places in mind that we can go to for our dates. First up, a little café that's down the road.

"All right, ready for your next little date?"

She peeks over her mug and lowers it a little. "I guess. Am I going to like it, at least?"

"Oh, yeah. It's gonna be the winner. Trust me. It's been a long time since I've done this, so I'm a little rusty."

She plays with her mug, then finally nods in agreement. "If you promise it's going to be fun, then let's go."

I want to clap my hands and jump for joy but refrain from doing so. I'm a grown ass adult who wants to go on this date more than anything. I reach for her hand and bring it to my lips. "I promise you'll love this one, and it's away from people."

Her shoulders drop with relief. Glad I made the right choice.

We return to the truck, passing shops with more bodies spilling out than before. The entire town has gotten busier. Good timing on our part to get a move on.

"I need to stop at the cabins first. You've gotta grab some warmer clothes."

Her head snaps so quickly to look at me, and I swear she reminds me of Regan from The Exorcist when her head rotates all the way around.

"Where the hell are you taking me?" She props her hands on her hips, raising one eyebrow.

I nervously laugh. I can't exactly tell her I spent some time at this place as a child. "I heard the locals talk about a place and want to check it out. Come on. Chop, chop."

"I'm not a goddamn dog," she grumbles.

Yes, well, I wasn't a liar until now.

I pull into her driveway first. "Grab your ski pants, mitts, toque, and maybe a better coat."

She groans. "I have a terrible feeling about this." She hops out of the truck.

I watch until she disappears inside. I reach for my phone, dialling Ma's number. It barely rings before she answers it.

"Hello, my dear son. Merry Christmas."

"Merry Christmas, Ma. Are you all ready for tomorrow?" I keep an eye on the door, waiting for Noel to reappear.

"Almost, just baking pies as we speak. Have a request?"

"Only apple, you know me. I wanted to let you know I'm bringing someone with me tomorrow."

She squeals into the phone. "About time, dear. I'm thrilled! Tell me about her."

"Her name is Noel—"

"Beautiful." She cuts me off.

"Right, anyway. I only wanted to check in and let you know the plans. I'll see you tomorrow. Love you."

"Love you too."

She sounds so excited that I'm bringing someone home. If that doesn't embarrass me, I couldn't tell you what would. Okay, maybe that one time I asked Claire Thompson out for the junior dance in front of the entire English class, and she told me I had a booger hanging out of my nose. That might be the most embarrassing moment of my life. The whole class laughed at me, and the gossip spread like wildfire that day. All she had to say was no and walked away, and I could have been spared.

That probably explains why I never dated until I was out of school. Even in college, I was leery about girls. I never fully trusted them. Some women are cunts. I'm just sayin'. It got worse once I started my own company, and they found out how much I was worth, hence why I haven't said anything to Noel yet.

"All right, your place now," Noel says as she hops in the cab.

She looks like an abominable snowman, bundled up extra warm. I lean in, getting closer to her lips.

"You look sexy like this. Too bad it'll take forever to reach that sweet pussy of yours now." I kiss her, moving back into my seat.

"I hate you so much right now."

"Yeah, you nice and wet for me?" I lower my voice.

She reaches over the seat, running her hand up my thigh, moving to my twitching dick. Her index finger lightly touches it. I groan on contact.

"You're playing with fire, Noel."

I ram the truck in reverse, forcing her back in her seat. Now I have to drive with a hard-on. I readjust my jeans, trying to make room. Noel's laugh fills the cab.

"Laugh it up, baby. I'll fuck you in the snow the first chance I get."

"You wouldn't dare."

I chuckle. "Challenge accepted, my dear, when you least expect it."

"It's not happening, North. I'm not freezing my fuckin' pussy off for you."

"I'll keep it warm, don't you worry." Now my hard-on is a full-blown ready-to-blow hard-on. The thought of fucking her in the snow, oh, it's definitely happening now.

11

Noel

I can't figure out why I had to dress in all of my winter gear. I can't see us skiing or snowboarding, especially on Christmas Eve, but they're the only outdoor activities that I know. He's in and out of his cabin faster than I was, looking way sexier than I do. I feel like the Grinch and look like a fuckin' Who.

He rubs his hands together when he takes his seat, looking like a kid in a candy shop.

"I'm so excited about this." His mischievous grin comes out.

I, on the other hand, am nervous about what's coming. "I'll let you know when we get to this mystery spot."

As we drive, I can't help but look at the scenery. When I drove up here, I was too busy keeping my eyes on the road. I didn't get to take any of this in. The mountains are so large that it's ridiculous to believe they even exist. No matter how many times I see them, they still take my breath away.

"They sure are beautiful, aren't they?" I ask North.

"They are. I miss them the most when I'm in the city."

Hold the goddamn phone! He lives in the city, too. This whole time, we could've crossed paths and never known it. I don't mention anything. He could've said something earlier, but he chose not to. He obviously doesn't want to get personal because this won't last forever. After tomorrow, I'm guessing we will go our separate ways.

Hopefully, my black heart doesn't get too attached. I don't think I'll get over it. I'm surprised I'm not crying over my ex, but honestly, that ship sailed long before he slept with my supposedly best friend. So there's that.

I most likely will get a visit from the douchebag when I get home, and I am not looking forward to it. I almost want to extend my stay here, but unfortunately, I have to head home on the twenty-seventh. I was lucky that I got this time off, especially during the Christmas break, so I can't push my luck.

"We're here." North's voice breaks into my thoughts.

I look around, and all I see is a field of white. I'm so confused. "Where is here, exactly?"

"That, I couldn't tell you. All I know is that it's the perfect place for what we're about to do." His hazel eyes sparkle in the sunlight. His dark brown hair curls around his ears from being pushed down from his toque. He looks so innocent that I have a terrible feeling about this.

He opens his door as I open mine. I'm greeted with silence, not even a whisper of wind. The snow is so thick on the trees that it silences any sound coming from any direction. I could spend hours out here listening to nothing. No cars driving by, honking or revving their engines, and no people yelling. Just no people in general. I tilt my head up to the sky, blue with no clouds. I close my eyes. I hear North approaching me with his boots crunching in the snow. When his hands wrap around my waist, I lean into him.

"I needed this, especially after this morning."

His nose touches my neck, and the coldness sends goosebumps down my arms. Then his warm breath heats me up. "I'm glad, baby. But I need you to get on the ground for me now."

My mind races, and that needy pussy wakes up. I shift slightly on my feet, tilting my head to look at him. "Why?" That's all I can muster up for a response because my brain isn't working right now.

"Snow angels. Why? What did you have in mind?" He raises an eyebrow in amusement.

I look back at the empty field. Snow angels. "Like what five-year-olds make?"

He walks me backwards, staring into my eyes. "Yes. Show me what you got, baby." Then he pushes me into the snow.

"This is the stupidest thing I've ever done." I'm currently lying like a starfish in the snow. Next to me, North is having the time of his life.

His legs and arms are swishing back and forth. "That's because you aren't even trying. What kind of angel are you?"

"I'm Lucy," I said deadpan, looking over at him.

"That's not funny." He stops rolling onto his side, looking at me. "You're not the fuckin' devil. Now swing those goddamn body parts for me."

I love it when he talks like this. I didn't think I would love it when a man gets all demanding. It's precisely what I'm looking for. I don't move a single muscle. I simply stare at him. He lets out a low growl, rolling on top of me. The air is almost knocked out of me.

"If you don't listen, then I guess I'll have to help you." He moves his hands on mine and wraps his feet around mine. “Now move.” He moves his arms and legs with mine.

He never takes his eyes off mine. Our breath mingles together as we create an angel together. My legs have to do most of the work, while his arms work on the wings. My legs are on fire, and I’m so out of breath.

“I can’t do it anymore,” I struggle to say.

He stops moving, propping himself up, taking the weight off my chest. “If you did it yourself the first time, it would’ve been easier, but I’ll admit this was amusing.” He lowers his lips to mine but doesn’t kiss me. “Now, are you going to be a good girl and create one on your own?”

“Yes.”

He presses his lips to mine, and a moan slips past mine. I want him so bad again. His lips are so soft against mine; I can’t think of anything else but kissing him. He makes the world disappear. He makes me want to be better.

When he pulls away, his smile is so bright. “Show me what you got, Grinch.”

I punch him in the ribs, and he laughs as he rolls off me. When he helps me stand, I look at our mangled angel. The wings look amazing, but the bottom? Not so much.

“It’s so ugly.” I can’t help but laugh at our zombie angel.

He tilts his head from right to left. “There’s room for improvement. Let’s try again, naked this time.” He unzips his coat, laying it on the snow.

"Are you kidding me?" I'm too shocked to stop him as he sits on his coat to pull his boots off.

"Live a little. No one is out here. It's like skinny dipping but in snow. Besides, we can warm each other up."

Oh my God, I can't believe I'm doing this. I unzip my coat and start undressing. The coldness nips at my body. I'm about to pull my shirt off when I look over at North, and he's standing only in his boxers. He runs his thumbs through the waistband.

"Hurry, it's freezing out here."

I roll my eyes. "You think!" I tear my shirt off, then pull my jeans down. With a deep breath, I unhook my bra, and the cold air hits my nipples. "This is so not fair." I slip my panties down and almost feel bad for North. If he did have a hard-on, it's long gone.

He grabs my hand, pulling me onto his coat. "We'll do it together on the count of three."

We turn around as he starts his countdown. *Three... Two...* He pulls me down, and I scream. It's so fucking cold.

"Work fast, baby," he demands, working my arm with his.

We build tandem snow angels naked on Christmas Eve.

12

North

That's the craziest thing I've ever done with a girl. I'll admit I wasn't thinking. Now, we are grabbing our clothes and running back to the truck. I open the back door, throw clothes in and help Noel in. She's a shivering mess but laughing nonetheless.

"Oh my God, I can't believe we did that." She's blowing in her hands, trying to warm them up.

I climb over the seat to start the truck, cranking the heat on high. "I can't either. Hanging around you makes me lose my mind."

"In a good way, right?" She looks at me when I sit next to her.

"Of course," I reassure her. "Come here. We need to warm up." Her body is shaking, and I wish I had a blanket in here.

"I don't think I ever want to do that again." She laughs. "Look at our angels. They have butt cheeks."

"Speak for yourself. I'm pretty sure mine has balls." I squint, looking closer out the window.

She pushes my hair out of my face when I look at her. Her smile finally reaches her eyes. She seems more relaxed out here. Her hand tugs at the chain around my neck, pulling me closer.

"Thank you for this. I needed it more than you know. She would've loved to meet you. You and she would've gotten into so much mischief together."

I don't even need to ask who she's talking about. I place my hand over her heart.

"She's right here every single day. She's with you in every decision you make. In your mind, you ask her what to do, and you already know what she would tell you. She hasn't left you, Noel."

Her forehead lowers to mine. "It's hard some days. All I want is to have a conversation with her. We could chat about nothing as long as I heard her voice one last time. I want to call her and ask about the most random, stupidest thing that only she would understand."

I rub her back, pulling her closer. I don't say anything else because I can't help. I've never lost a parent, so I don't know what she's going through. I've only ever lost grandparents. It still hurts, but it's a different kind of hurt.

"Should we get dressed? We can head back to my cabin. I'll make us some food."

"Mmm, that would be wonderful. At least this way, I won't burn myself." She holds up her hand that she burnt this morning.

"Does it still hurt?"

"No, it's totally fine, especially after the snow angels. That's a lot of ice."

I pass her her clothes so we can get a move on. This day is almost over, and tomorrow is going to be the make or break of this arrangement.

When we reach my cabin, I quickly build a fire. The cold has worked its way deep into our bones. The crackling of the fire makes the cabin feel like home. This was where I first learned how to build a fire. I was so scared. I thought I was going to burn the entire cabin down.

I watch as she makes herself at home on the couch that my entire family still sits on from time to time. She looks like she belongs here. I give my head a shake. I can't be having these thoughts. I hand her the remote for the TV. "It has to be something Christmassy, or I take this back."

"Are you serious?" She grips the remote, tugging when I don't let go.

"Like a heart attack. My favourite movie is Home Alone." I wink at her before I let go and head to the kitchen. I can hear her mumbling to herself until the TV turns on. Home Alone is a safe movie for someone who doesn't like Christmas. It's not even centred on Christmas.

I make us something simple, tomato soup and grilled cheese sandwiches. It's comfort food, really. When I make my way back into the living room, she's curled up under a blanket watching, you guessed it, Home Alone. I smile as I place the food on the coffee table.

I pass her a bowl. "Good movie?"

"Don't be an ass. Of course, it is. Who wouldn't want to kick adults' asses when you're a kid."

"I just want to know who cleans the house because Kevin did not. There's no way." I sit beside her and grab some blankets, moving closer.

"I only want to know what his dad does for a living because that house, that many kids, and a trip to Paris. Drug dealer." She shrugs her shoulders.

We eat in silence while watching our movie, but my mind keeps wandering to her naked body in the snow. My dick twitches with the thought of her nipples tightening from the cold. I grab her dish, setting it on the table before I flick the blanket off us.

"I've been waiting all day. I need you right now." I crawl over her and grab her hair, pulling her head back and exposing her neck. Running my nose along her nape, I trace her pulse with my tongue. Her little moans edge me on. "You're so pretty when you moan for me."

I guide my other hand under her shirt, freeing her breast from her bra. Pinching her tight nipple, her hips buck into me.

"North," she moans.

I finally place my lips on hers, kissing her deeply. Her hand works its way into my hair. God, it feels so good. I pull back, sitting up.

"I have a better idea, baby. I want you to put on a show for me."

Her eyes grow large. "A show? What kind of show?"

I lift my eyebrow and grin. "A one-woman kind of show. Get up the stairs to the bedroom before I catch you."

I stand, waiting for her to move. I snap my fingers for her to get moving, and she stumbles off the couch, falling on the floor. I patiently wait for her to get upright, and then she takes off. I follow behind, calling out the directions to my room.

I watch as she crawls onto my bed. This room had never seen a woman in it before, and thank god I don't have it decorated like I did as a teenager, with half-naked women on the walls. Then she flicks open her jeans. Now I want to say the next part was the sexiest thing I've seen, but it's Noel and well...

She falls off the bed while trying to kick her jeans off.

"Ouch! Fuck. North, this was a horrible idea."

I can't help but laugh. "You could've undressed standing up." I rush over to help her up off the floor.

"I was trying to be sexy for you," she grits out, rubbing her ass. She finishes taking her pants off, along with her shirt. She stands, wearing only her bra and panties.

I move closer to her, running my hand up her thigh. "Are you ready to show me how you play with yourself?"

"Yes."

I smack her ass, watching her pupils dilate. I'm sure if I touched her pussy it would be soaking wet. I watch as she climbs on the bed again, her hands working behind her back. Her bra falls down her breasts. I want to touch them so badly, but I pull the chair from my desk and sit, waiting for the show to begin.

13

Noel

My heart is racing. North is sitting in the chair, watching, waiting for me. The only time I touch myself is in private. I'm not sure what to do. Will he judge me? I usually watch porn when I do this.

"What's wrong?"

"I'm not used to an audience." I stare into his eyes, waiting for him to say something.

"Want me to guide you?" He unzips his pants, pulling out his hard cock.

All I can do is nod.

"Take your panties off and lie back."

I do what he says. The sound of spit makes my pussy clench.

"I need you desperate for me, desperate for me to fuck you after. Can you do that for me?" His voice is husky and low.

"I can do that for you," I manage to say.

"Perfect. Now, take those hands and slowly run them up your body. Feel how soft your body is. I want you to cup your breasts."

My hands glide over my stomach, sending goosebumps all over. My entire body lights up when I move my hands to my breasts. I don't think I have been this turned on before. I'm so wet it's like a river between my legs.

His voice grows rougher. "I want you to pinch your sensitive nipples. Imagine my hands touching you, pinching your nipples."

I moan louder than expected, feeling the electricity shoot to my pussy and make my toes curl.

"Now, spread your legs. Show me that pussy of yours. I want to see it."

I spread my legs open for him, which results in a growl.

"Wider. I want to see everything."

I hear the sounds of him stroking himself, and I so badly want to open my eyes, but I'm afraid it'll take away from this fantasy of him touching me.

"Mmm, better. Now stick two fingers in your mouth and suck them, suck them like they are my cock."

I lift my fingers to my mouth, sticking them in and sucking on them. I do imagine it's his cock. I moan around my fingers and hear him groan again from his seat.

"Good girl. Take one finger and place it deep inside of you."

My core is wet when I outline my entrance. I slowly enter, moaning as I go.

"Now fuck yourself, nice and slow. In and out."

I do as he says, going slowly, feeling my muscles tighten around my finger with each stroke. My heels dig into the bed, and the room fills with our deep breathing.

"Tease yourself. I don't want you to come just yet. I want to hear how wet you are. I want to hear you moan and whimper. Let me hear you," North orders me.

I work myself so much that all you can hear is my fingers slipping in and out, and my breathing picks up when he speaks again.

"Add another finger, fuck yourself faster and make yourself come. Come for me, baby."

I shove another finger inside, following his orders, moaning. With my other hand, I pinch my nipple and grind my hips. "Oh, God." My body is on fire. I'm so close to coming when hands touch mine, pulling mine away.

"I'll take over from here." He moves between my legs, lining his cock with my core and slowly pushing in. "Fuck, you feel good." He pushes the rest of the way in. "I can feel you squeezing me." He groans.

He sits there, so still. I'm getting frustrated. He interrupted my orgasm for this. I move my hips, shamelessly fucking him, and his finger finally moves to my clit, rubbing it so gently. My fingers claw at the blanket as I squeeze my muscles around his shaft.

"Yes, baby. Fuck me. I can tell that you're close."

Then he slams his hips into me. My back arches off the bed. "North." His name slips past my lips. His fingers are skilled, just like his fucking cock. He sits me up so I look into his face and grips my throat.

"Come for me, baby," he grinds out.

His other hand works my hips into his, fucking me harder. His moans send me over the top. I come so hard as I fall back on the bed. He kisses my stomach, then my breasts, and finally my lips.

"Hey, thanks for the show."

I cover my face. "I can't believe I did that. You bring out some kind of a freak in me."

He removes my hands from my face, his face never giving anything away. "A freak in the bed is the best kind; it's always the innocent ones you have to watch out for." He bops me on the nose before getting out of bed. I watch as he leaves, his tight, beautiful ass the last thing I see.

I wake up in the middle of the night in a sweat. The room is pitch black. The only sound is North's light snoring. I gently get out of bed, grabbing his shirt off the floor. I make my way down the stairs. The Christmas tree lights are on, illuminating the living room in a multitude of colours. I add another log to the fire, heating the space. The crackling has become one of my new favourite sounds. I'm going to miss it when I leave.

Taking a seat on the couch, I grab the blanket. The stupid dream keeps replaying in my mind, one that I can't get rid of ever since walking into my boyfriend's bedroom. Sorry, ex-boyfriend. I can feel my heart clench in my chest, feeling the heartbreak all over again. I thought we were in love. I thought we were going to be growing old together. I didn't see any signs whatsoever that he was stepping out on me. Not once did he say he was working late or wanted to hang out with his friends. I keep wondering how they made time for each other.

I don't get it. Am I that horrible of a person that even my best friend wants to hurt me? We've been friends since college. She never appeared to be a jealous type. When I got with my ex, maybe I noticed some changes. She hung around more and always invited herself over. If anything, I would blame her more than him. But he could've stopped it at any time. I can't believe I was so blind!

I curl deeper into the blanket, watching the fire. The flames dance around the room. Then it finally dawned on me. It's Christmas Day.

"Merry Christmas, Mom," I whisper into the quietness of the night. "I hope it's festive wherever you are right now because it's very dark and dreary down here. I met someone who's been trying his hardest to get me to enjoy it, but honestly, I don't think it's helping. I don't have the heart to tell him. I can't break his spirit. I can't be that person. What should I do, Mom?"

I feel so bad for North. All these dates with him being romantic, and he still can't get me to enjoy Christmas. At this point, I honestly think I'm broken.

I'm trying. I swear I am. Maybe today, with his family, I'll feel a little spark.

14
North

I felt her leave the bed halfway through the night. I wanted to follow, but deep inside, she needed to be alone. Today is going to be a hard one for both of us. She will be introduced to a family that thinks we've been dating for months, and I will watch everyone fall in love with her. I was lying in bed, listening to nothing, when I heard her talk. I stay put as much as I want to creep out there and listen. You know what they say about eaves-droppers. Nothing good comes from it.

I wake sometime later with a grunt. My body can't handle these cold mornings anymore. That's how you know you're getting closer to your thirties. Everything is shutting down. When I roll over, her bedside is empty and cold. No matter how much I want to sleep in, I do have to get a move on. Sliding out of bed, I grab a pair of plaid PJ pants.

I look over the stair railing and see Noel sleeping on the couch. I quietly make my way to the kitchen to start a pot of coffee. The cabin fills with the scent of coffee in no time.

"North, it's too early to be up," Noel rasps out. All I see from the couch is her hand waving at me.

I walk over to her, grabbing her hand to kiss her palm. "Nonsense, sweet cheeks. The sun's up, so we should be up. We're wasting the day away already." I so badly want to wish her a Merry Christmas, but I hold back. The puffiness of her eyes tells me it's not the time. "Come on. Coffee should be ready."

"What time do we have to head to your parents?"

"Afternoon. They're all excited. My mother squealed on the phone when I told her about my bringing home a date."

She groans when she sits up. "You're kidding? They aren't going to make a big deal about this, are they? I don't want it to be hard on you after the fact. We haven't talked about the after."

I haven't put much thought into it if I'm being honest. I was hoping we never had this talk. I guess that's naïve of me or extremely hopeful of the future. Here I am, being too optimistic again.

"I'll just tell them it didn't work out, the old classic break-up story." I shrug my shoulders before turning back to the coffee.

"I don't want you taking the heat for me. Blame me so you don't look bad to your family."

"I can't do that. They'll see how nice you are and won't believe that for a second, and besides, I have to protect your honour." I pass her a mug of black coffee and two sugars. I pick up on these things.

Our fingertips brush when she takes it from me. I feel that spark, the one I've never felt with anyone else before.

"Honestly, my honour is the last thing you'll have to worry about."

I hold her eyes. "I worry a lot about you already, Noel. I worry that today is going to break you, and I won't be able to fix it."

I watch as her eyes glimmer with tears. "Don't do this; you barely know me," she pleads.

"I can still care about you. If today gets to be too much, give me a safe word."

She scoffs. "Like what, fruit cake?"

"Perfect! That shit is nasty, anyway. I'm gonna get dressed. Then we'll head to your cabin so you can get dressed because if I have to look at you in my shirt for much longer, I don't think we'll be making it for Christmas dinner still looking like perfect little angels." I glance down at her legs before returning to her eyes.

"I'm sure your mom knows you aren't an angel."

I place my hand over my heart. "I was an angel until you came along."

"Mmm-hmm. And I was a virgin."

I place my mug on the counter and creep forward, wrapping my arm around her waist. "Is your ass a virgin?" I ask in her ear as my other hand glides down, grabbing her ass cheek. "Because I have some not-so-angel-like things I would like to do to it."

Her hands wrap in my hair and tug my head back. Her lips trace my neck, running to my ear. "My entire body isn't a virgin." She nips my earlobe.

I groan, pressing her into my hard-on. The thought of bending her over the counter and fucking her ass runs through my head faster than I can admit. I'll come in my pants if I don't step away now. Then it'll be a white Christmas, for sure. Swallowing hard, I step back.

"You're an evil woman." I massage my cock just for her. "I'll be upstairs if you need me."

"Think of me in that cold shower, sweet cheeks."

I turn to see her smirking at me. Then she winks and licks her lips. I can't take it much longer. I need that cold shower because I don't think my dick can grow much more.

"I'm going to feel so underdressed. You realize this, right?" Noel runs her hands along her jeans for the tenth time since getting dressed.

"You look sexy as fuck; I wouldn't worry. You didn't know you would be spending Christmas with anyone, and I didn't think about getting you an outfit for today. We're both equally guilty."

"Spoken from the ass that's dressed like a model."

"I can change into jeans if you want."

"I don't want to be that couple, but can't you look like a slob for once?" She laughs.

When I came down the stairs earlier, I was greeted by a slack-jawed Noel. I went from lumberjack redneck to CEO in a matter of minutes. I was dressed in black slacks and a white dress shirt with a Christmas tie. Then she panicked because she didn't pack anything that would look nice. Honestly, what she's wearing is perfect. Her jeans and a red off the shoulder sweater are sexy as hell. She looks great in red. I haven't told her the worst part yet, but I'll wait until we get to my parents. I need her to show up and not jump ship.

She's wearing her hair down in light curls. I want to run my hands through them and grab a handful. Later, I tell myself. We always have later.

"I've been a slob this entire time. You look beautiful, trust me."

She mumbles to herself, folding her hands in her lap. "Is there anything I should know about your family before I meet them? We also need to work on our story."

"Our story is we met one incredible day while you were out in the snow. You didn't like me the first time but couldn't resist my charm when I returned the second time."

She scoffs. "Yeah, okay. Is that what you tell yourself at night?"

I turn onto the main road into town. "It is. You were beautiful, even in all of your snow gear. I'm glad I came back, Noel. I'm also glad you didn't turn out to be an old lady."

"Not into an age-gap relationship, sonny boy?"

"I wouldn't get these intelligent conversations, that's for sure, but no, Noel. I wouldn't have met the best person who crossed my path in a long time."

I can feel her eyes on me. She doesn't say anything. I don't expect her to. It's a lot to take in. I pretty much just laid my heart out to her.

Pulling onto my parents' street has my heart doing something else. I don't think I'm ready for this.

15

Noel

Oh, mother fucking cheez-its, this man and his words. He's so smooth with them. It's not even funny. I'm so busy staring at him, trying to think of a reply, that I haven't even noticed we are parked.

"We're here." He tilts his head to the front window of the truck.

I finally turn my head and immediately gasp. I was expecting an average modern house, not this huge, monstrous place. This can't be right, can it? I get they are retired, but retired from what? I should've asked more questions, but does it really matter?

"Holy shit, North. Now I feel under-dressed." My heart skips a beat. He grabs my hand.

"I promise you. You aren't. Trust me." He hops out and grabs all the gifts that he bought. I do the same, grabbing the ones I purchased. I hope his parents like the one I got for them.

Walking up the stairs, the front deck is decorated with Christmas decorations, and a wreath hangs on the door. It looks familiar. I just can't place where I've seen it. The door swings open to a thrilled woman.

"Oh my, Merry Christmas, North." The woman pulls him in for a hug. He has to bend down so she can wrap her arms around his neck.

Then she turns to me, and I don't have time to move. She embraces me so hard the air in my lungs evaporates.

"I'm so glad he finally brought someone home for Christmas. I got worried there for a while, and you know how it is. The last child—"

"Okay, Ma, that's enough," North cuts in. "Can we at least make introductions first before you embarrass me?"

"Right, sorry, sweetheart." She releases me, and I take a deep breath in.

"That's all right. I'm Noel Tinsley."

"I take it North never mentioned anyone's name."

I turn to North for help.

"You know, it's always Ma and Pops. Noel, this is Ella."

This is shit we should've figured out before coming here. Our cover is going to be blown before dinner is even fuckin' served.

"That's all right. David and James are in the den. I'm not sure where Summer and Blake are. They are probably trying to fight with Asher while Hanna relaxes."

I'm trying to remember these names; I can figure out to whom they belong. I'm guessing James is his brother, Summer is his sister, and Blake is the brother-in-law who wears the douche loafers—got it.

Walking inside the house takes my breath away again. It opens to the grand living room and kitchen. The ceilings are high and vaulted. A brick fireplace entirely takes up one wall, with windows on either side letting in natural light. A massive Christmas tree is tucked away in a corner with a huge pile of gifts underneath. My gaze takes everything in, and Christmas is everywhere. A snowman and several Santas stand around the base of the fireplace, and a garland hangs on almost every available surface. I'm so busy taking in the sights that I don't realize North has grabbed my bags.

Ella comes back to us, holding a wrapped package. "You know the drill, North." I stare at this wrapped gift in horror. What drill? I look back at North and see sympathy in his eyes.

"Sorry, baby, but it's tradition."

"What is?" I whisper.

He tears into the paper, only to hold up two matching ugly Christmas sweaters. I bite my lip and shake my head no. He dips his chin.

"Come on, and I'll show you the bathroom." He leads me to the loveliest bathroom I have ever seen, but even here, Christmas barfed everywhere. He closes the door behind him. "I'm sorry. I was going to tell you, but I needed you to show up."

"Yeah, well, a little heads up would've been nice. A goddamn Christmas sweater? Seriously? I can't believe this is happening." I rip the stupid sweater from his hands and cringe. It's a goddamn reindeer with ornaments on it. "North, what the hell is this?"

"Rudolph?" He shrugs. "I really am sorry. We all have to wear them. It makes her happy. Even Pops wears one."

I tear my sweater off and place on this god-awful one. I look at myself in the mirror. Then North stands beside me in his matching sweater, and I laugh.

"How many do you own?"

"Don't tell her, but I donate them yearly, or my closet would overflow with them. Come on, my sexy reindeer, let's head out before they think we're doing more than changing."

I smack his ass. "Is that all you think about?"

He turns to look at me. "With you, yes."

And now my panties are wet. *Fuck.*

I have to remember I'm at his parent's house, and we can't get into trouble, no matter how much I want to jump his bones. He makes an ugly sweater look hot as fuck. It's not fair. He could probably turn a burlap sack into something drool-worthy.

I immediately followed him out of the bathroom to be greeted by his entire family. If my cheeks weren't red before, they are on fire now. Not how I wanted to meet everyone. I alternate a hand on each cheek, trying to cool them off. North squeezes my hand.

"Everyone, this is Noel, my girlfriend."

That is the first time we use the term girlfriend, fake or not. It sounds too good coming out of his mouth.

"Hello, everyone. Thank you for having me today."

"To be honest, I was beginning to think lil' bro here was gay. He never dated anyone, too afraid of his fortune or some bullshit," his brother James says.

North stiffens next to me, so I run my hand along his arm. I can't relate to what it's like to have siblings, but I imagine this teasing is usual.

"Yes, well, at least I own my own company. You can't say the same, now, can you?"

I try to keep my facial expression neutral, but that's fuckin' news to me. I know he said he loved his job, but to own it? Good on him. That's been my goal since I could remember. If only I could figure out how to get there, I would quit my stupid job in a heartbeat. Maybe I would be happier in life if I just did more of what I wanted to and less of what was expected.

"I'm not afraid, unlike you. I'm surprised you had the balls to bring your girlfriend home."

"All right, that's enough from you two." The booming voice of their father breaks them up. "For the life of me, I can't figure out where this is coming from suddenly?"

James scoffs before leaving the kitchen. All the other members watch him walk off before turning back to me. I'm unsure if I did something wrong by being here, but I suddenly need to find an exit.

16
North

I was basking in the happiness of watching Noel wear a Christmas sweater, only for that bubble to burst once my brother started in on his usual talk; he's always been jealous of my company. He had a chance to go in with me, but his wife talked him out of it. She thought it would be the worst idea ever and that I wouldn't make a thing. Little did they know that I turned it into a multi-million-dollar company in only a few short years, and they are still pissed. They expect me to help them and act as if I owe them. Sorry, but I don't. I worked my ass off to build my company, not you.

Now, Noel knows I own a company. She kept her shit together, acting like she knew this entire time, so I'll give it to her, but wait until someone slips the name or how much it's worth. Then what? I don't think she'll be like every other woman out there. She doesn't seem to be snobby, especially after all those dates I took her on. She loved those.

"Son, perhaps you should show Noel the rest of the house," Pops suggests.

"That's a wonderful idea. Summer and Hanna can help me in the kitchen," Ma says, waving for my sister and Hanna to follow. They give Noel a small smile when they pass her.

I take Noel's hand, leading her up the stairs. "Sorry about my brother. He's a real piece of work."

"It's okay. I'm an only child, so I never knew what it was like to grow up with siblings. Now I know I'm not missing anything at all."

"God, no. Sometimes it's even worse. At least this time, we didn't throw any fists."

"Jesus," she mutters.

I walk to my room that I stay in when I come to visit. Ma decorated it in muted tones, and luckily for Noel, there were no Christmas decorations.

"You'll be safe here for a little while. I can't guarantee how dinner will go over, but I'll make sure to place you far away from James."

"I'm sure I can handle him. I used to bartend in a questionable establishment, so he'll be a breeze."

She lies on the bed, closing her eyes. It feels weird having her here, especially in a bed in my parent's house while they are downstairs. Usually, this would happen when you're a teenager. I sit on the edge, leaning my elbows on my knees.

"You're quiet. What are you thinking?"

I laugh. "How I never brought home any girl, even when I was a teenager. Does that make me weird?"

She sits up. "Nah. If it makes you feel better, I didn't date until I was out of high school. I didn't lose my virginity until I was eighteen. I'm sure I was the weird one in my school."

"Eighteen, eh? We must be made for each other because that's when I lost mine, but it was a drunken night, and I wanted to get it over with. I don't even remember the chick's name."

"North, the first time is meant to be special."

"Why, though? I never understood that. Why does it matter who gets to claim it? It's not a prize to be won; it's mine to give how I choose, correct?"

"I guess. I never thought of it that way. I guess some girls are more attached to it than others."

"Was your night special?" I honestly can't believe we are having this conversation. Of all the conversations to have, this is the one.

She laughs, then cringes. "It was, um... a drunk night. I turned eighteen, hit the bar for the first time, and found some guy." She covers her face, laughing. "It was horrible."

"Yet, you get mad at me, telling me it's supposed to be special."

She throws a pillow at me. "Hey, it happened on my birthday. That was special."

I grab the pillow and throw it back at her. "Did you come at least?"

"No. I don't even think he did." She furrows her brows in thought.

I pull her ankle, dragging her closer to me. I lean in closer to her face. "That's sad. Should we pretend we're both virgins and have a do over?"

"With your family downstairs?"

"You'll have to be silent." I undo her jeans, moving onto my knees so I can drag them off. "Can you be a good girl and do that for me?"

"I think so."

That's not good enough for me. I work under my shirt for my tie, and when I finally undo it, I slip it off. I pull her panties off next, rolling them into a ball. "Open for me." When her mouth opens, I shove her panties inside. "Now, I know you'll be quiet. Give me your hands." I pull her hands above her head and tie them to the headboard.

Moving her sweater up, I work a breast out of her bra. The cool air hardens her nipple. She shifts under me, pressing into my raging erection—such a tease. Two can play that game. I take her nipple into my mouth, sucking hard before I bite it. The room is filled with her muffled moans. I want to take my precious ass time, but I can't.

Sitting up, I undo my pants, digging into my pocket to grab the condom. I might have pre-thought this out beforehand. Sliding my pants and boxers down, I tear open the condom wrapper with my teeth, watching Noel the entire time. I spread her legs wider, allowing her to wrap her legs around mine.

"You're so sexy, gagged and bound like this." I line my cock up to her pussy. "Ready to be fucked fast and hard?" All she can do is nod. I slam into her without warning, making her back buck off the bed. Her pussy is so fucking warm.

"That's right, baby. Squeeze my fucking cock with your pussy. Make me come. I need to feel every single inch of you." I grab her hips, never giving her any room to spare. I move my fingers to her clit, rubbing her sensitive bud.

"I need you to come, baby." I watch as her hands grip the headboard, her head dipping back, her chin towards the ceiling. Her muscles clench around my cock. "Yes, baby, like that." I fuck her until I spill into the condom. I reach up and take her panties from her mouth.

"Jesus, North," she pants.

"I'll admit, I never fucked like that when losing my virginity. I think I was a two-pump kind of guy."

We both laugh. I kiss her lips as I untie her hands.

"Well, thank god you aren't like that anymore. But we probably should be getting back to your family."

I groan. "I suppose before they think about what we're up to."

Her face goes a bright shade of red. "Oh my God, they are going to know I just had sex with their son in their family home." She covers her face.

"Come on. It won't be that bad." I sit up and pass her pants back to her.

"I hate you so much. I look like I've just been fucked."

I grin. "I know. That's the best part. Welcome to the family, girlfriend."

17

Noel

I try to make myself look decent, all while North laughs at me. It's not fair how guys don't even look like they just had their brains fucked out of their heads. My hair is a mess. I try to finger comb it, but I shortly give that up.

"You look beautiful. Stop worrying so much."

"That's easy for you to say. You don't even look like we did anything. Are you even sure you came?"

He laughs. "Trust me. I came all right."

He takes my hand, leading me into the hallway. I take my time looking around this time. I take in all the family photos, a little North growing up through the years with his siblings. My eyes land on the very last photo, the frame with their last name, a familiar last name. It's a popular last name, so I don't think much of it.

We find his mom in the kitchen still. I feel guilty that I didn't offer to help earlier, but cooking isn't my strong suit. Dad and I would always go out to a restaurant for any major holiday. I feel even worse knowing Dad's at home alone today. I'm horrible.

"I'm sorry, Ella. Could I help with anything?" I ask when we reach her.

She looks up at me and smiles. "Oh, gosh, no. You're the guest. Grab an eggnog and take a seat." She dances around the kitchen, working around Summer and Hannah. It's a beautiful sight. I wonder if this is how Mom would look if she were still here. I look away before the tears form. North meets my eyes and cups my cheek.

"Don't, please," I whisper. Because if he asks how I'm doing, I'll start crying for sure. He simply nods and lets me walk away. I find his dad in the living room, along with his nephew.

"Noel, sit, please. How's your Christmas so far?"

I do as he says. Christmas music softly plays over the TV. "It's going lovely. Thank you for having me."

"It's our pleasure, anything for North. He deserves it, especially after what he's been through."

What has he been through? North doesn't talk about himself. He's a complete mystery that I haven't been able to crack open. His dad must be able to read my face because he keeps talking.

"Ever since starting his company, it hasn't been easy on him. His brother has been the jealous type, if you haven't noticed. It caused a huge riff between them. It's been hard on him, being this young and owning a multi-million-dollar company."

Hold the phone. Wait what? I swing my head to North, watching him laugh with his mom and sister. This laid-back man is worth that much? I don't believe it. There's no way. Why wouldn't he tell me? I told him so much about my life. I opened up the darkest parts, and he couldn't even give me an ounce of the truth. My heart slowly breaks even more just when I start to feel something for him. I understand this was a very short arrangement, so maybe we never should've slept together. We should've made rules of some sort.

I look back at his dad and smile. "I'm sure his luck has turned around now."

He pats my hand. "That it has. I haven't seen him this happy in years. Usually, he's grumpy around Christmas and hates coming home. I owe you a thank you for bringing him home and making him this happy."

"Me? I didn't do much. I can promise you that." I wouldn't think to classify North as grumpy on Christmas Day, but when I see his family with significant others, I can see why he would be. I'm glad I can make his day so happy. If only his dad didn't bring mine down even more.

"Dinner is ready." His Mom calls.

"Come, my dear, let's prepare for the madness." He grabs Asher's hand, helping him to the dining room.

North meets me halfway, reaching for my hand. "Have a good chat with Pops?"

I hum. "I did. He's a nice man. You're very loved by him. You know that?"

"That's because I'm the baby of the family. He finally got it right."

He pulls my chair out for me, and I'm thankful to be sitting next to Summer. She seems laid back, just like he is. She gently elbows me.

"Don't worry about James. He permanently has a stick shoved up his ass," she jokes.

I glance across the table only to see James glaring at us. I guess he doesn't like his sister joking about him or my being here. I'm not sure which.

The food gets passed around, and I'm overwhelmed by how much there is. It's been years since I've seen a Christmas dinner such as this. Everybody talks, shares inside jokes, and laughs at the stupidest shit.

I can only sit here and eat, mashing my potatoes even more. I keep replaying the conversation with his dad from earlier. North owns his own company, a multi-million-dollar one, to be exact. Then it hits me. His goddamn last name is Bradford. Bradford Industries. My fork freezes in my potatoes. I work for Bradford Industries as an accounting clerk. Oh my God. North is my boss's boss.

I angle my head slightly to get a good look at him. This entire time, and yet he doesn't look familiar. I never once looked into who owned the company I work at. I assumed it was an old fat guy living in the States, like most of our oilfield companies. I didn't think it was a hot guy.

He turns to look at me. "You all right? You've been quiet."

"I'm good," I squeak out.

He narrows his eyes. "If it gets to be too much, let me know, and we can sneak out." He wiggles his brows.

Yep, I doubt I'll be doing that again now that I know who he is. Does that make me a complete bitch? I can't sleep with my boss. Once he finds out, then what? I only have to keep this quiet until Christmas ends, our deal is done, and we go our separate ways.

"So, Noel. What is it you do for work?" James asks me glaringly.

I smile at him. "I work as an accounting clerk."

He nods, then looks at his brother and smirks. "And how long have you been dating my brother?"

"Why all the questions, James?" North's voice was harsh.

He gives us a half-cocked smile. "I'm only ensuring she isn't robbing you, dear brother."

North's body stiffens again.

"I can assure you, James, that I am not after your brother's money. I do have a job. Hence I have my own money, thank you very much. I would appreciate it if you stopped talking to me like I'm a money-hungry bitch. Please excuse my language." I go back to eating, and the entire table stays quiet.

North's hand lands on my thigh, squeezing it. If he didn't know how I felt about him, he does now. I don't want his money even though he doesn't know that I know about it.

Jesus, I'm confused.

18

North

I'm going to kill James. My secret is slowly unravelling, and soon Noel will know it. This supper needs to end. This was a horrible idea. Maybe I should've just told her the truth. This would be so much easier. Of all things to do, she didn't need to be defending herself against him. I should've put him in his place, but she jumped in so quickly I didn't have a chance.

"James, that's enough. Why must you turn everything into an argument? Can't we just have a lovely day?" Ma tells him.

He rolls his eyes and goes back to eating. The tension around the table doesn't lessen either—what a great way of trying to get Noel to fall in love with Christmas again.

Today was supposed to be a happy day. If I wanted to be grumpy, I would've come alone like always.

"I'm sorry, Noel. James here must have forgotten his manners. We usually don't talk to our guests with such rudeness."

"That's okay, Ella. I'm used to it." She smiles at Ma. "My ex-boyfriend loved to talk a lot of smack."

"Well, you got lucky with my brother. He's a huge softy," Summer says.

Noel presses her lips in a tight line. I would like to know what she's thinking.

"Here, Ma, let me help ya." I grab the plates from her hands and place them in the sink.

"You don't need to help me. I can do it."

I slowly narrow my eyes. "You cooked. I think I can handle a few dishes. Go relax until it's time for gifts."

She kisses my cheek. "You were always my favourite."

"You're only saying that because I'm cleaning."

She hitches her shoulder. "Perhaps. I'll send Noel in."

I get busy stacking dishes and scraping food into the garbage when Noel comes into the kitchen tugging at her sweater.

"When can I change?"

"When we get home. We all suffer together, remember?"

"I hate this. Give me the stupid plate," Noel snarls, snapping her hand in my face.

I push her hand down. "What's gotten into you? You've been in a mood since dinner. Was it what James said? Because if it was, please just ignore it. He's a dick."

"It's not that. Don't worry about it." She grabs the plate and loads it in the dishwasher. She ignores me the entire time.

I go about my business, leaving her alone as she wants. Ma watches us for a little while, and I want to take Noel into my arms and show the entire family that we are indeed in a relationship. I have a feeling she would punch the shit out of me if I tried right now.

Summer yells for everyone to meet in the living room for the opening of gifts, and I've never been more nervous than I am right now. This is the moment when Noel will experience the full-blown Christmas effect in the house. The gift exchange is a huge deal, another thing I should've warned her about. My bad.

I try to take her hand, but she pulls away from me. My heart drops to my feet. She has never once rejected me, not even in the beginning. I act as if nothing happened and sit on the couch next to her, making sure not to touch her. Pops makes his way to the mantle and grabs the Santa boot. I see Noel look at him, then at the boot.

I lean over to whisper in her ear. "He draws names to see who gets their gift first."

We watch carefully, praying that he pulls Asher's name first. When he pulls out the piece of paper and unfolds it, he locks eyes with Noel. She grips my hand in a tight hold.

"North, I don't want any gifts. Please, I can't do this," her voice shrinking.

When Pops hands her a small gift, and she doesn't move to take it, I reach for it, meeting his eyes, concern laced in them. I place the gift in her lap while he returns to picking names from the boot. Gifts begin to pile up in front of me while I try to comfort Noel. Everyone has opened their presents while we sit here.

"We can take them home with us if you don't want to open them in front of everyone."

"You can open yours. I'll be fine." She smiles at me before looking at the small gift in her lap again.

Asher's laugh rings loud in the room. "Tanks Uncle Norf. I loves it." He runs his wooden car along the floor.

"You're welcome, buddy." I take a gift bag in front of me. The café shop logo that Noel and I visited on our date yesterday was stamped all over it. I look for a gift tag.

To: North

From: Noel, Thank you for making this Christmas special. I'll never forget it.

I turn to look at her, but she's watching Asher play with his toy. I turn back to the bag, pulling out the travel mug I had been looking at. It's nothing fancy, just a plain black mug with the saying "*Coffee makes me poop*" on it. I thought it was hilarious. It's literally the perfect gift.

"Oh, Noel, you didn't have to get us anything." Ma breaks through my thoughts.

She's holding up a handcrafted cabin that looks almost like the one we own. It's beautiful.

"It looks just like the one we own," Pops says.

"You own a cabin?"

Shit, shit, shit.

"Oh, the Mountain Escape Cabins. That's ours," James says smugly.

"I'm sorry, yours?" Noel looks at him, confused.

"Yeah, it's the family's business. We own the big cabin and rent out all the smaller ones."

Her head swings to mine, and I cringe. "That's news you didn't bother to tell me, dear," she whisper-shouts.

I half-turn to face her and lower my voice. "We'll discuss it later."

If I could wrap this Christmas up in one word, *fucked* would be the word. I'm up shits creek without a paddle because I don't think I'm getting out of this without some good explanation—I honestly don't know how she's going to take it.

From the way she's shifting away from me, I'm going to say, not the best. I guess it'll be easy to tell the family how we broke up, and I can blame it on James.

Merry fuckin' Christmas.

19

Noel

It's just been one lie after another. It's not like North owes me explanations. It's fake dating without any commitment, after all. I guess I set the bar a little too high. I have to sit through everyone opening their presents while I hold on to this small, wrapped gift. I don't want to open it. It's from his parents, guaranteed to be something too lovely for me and something I don't deserve. I'm counting down the minutes when I can finally tear this sweater off and get out that front door. Finally, the last person opens their gift.

"Sorry, Ma, but Noel and I are going to head out. I have to head home tomorrow." He stands to hug his Mom and then his Dad.

I stand, moving to his Mom. "Thank you again for having me. It was a wonderful dinner." She pulls me in for another hug.

"I'm so grateful you came. Thank you." She pulls me away to kiss me on the cheek. She places her hand on my cheek and looks me in the eyes. I swallow hard. It's been a very long time since a mother has embraced me. I give her a quick nod before stepping back.

"Thank you, Noel. I hope to see you again," his dad says before embracing me in a quick hug.

I don't say anything; I can't lie to him. He doesn't deserve that. He's too nice of a person to be hurt. I grab my things and wait for North by the door. I'll admit that, save for his brother, and I did enjoy the day. His family is very welcoming. I don't think lying to them was worth it because the look on his parent's faces isn't worth the lie. They look so happy to see North with someone finally.

"Bye, son. I'll see you in the new year."

"See ya, Pops. Ma, love you. Thanks again." He hugs her before coming over to me. "Ready?"

"Yep. Bye, guys." I wave to his family for the last time.

The ride to the cabins is quiet. I haven't said a word. I'm trying to figure out how to tell him that I know who he is.

If his dad had never mentioned it, I'm not sure I would've figured it out. His truck is from the '90s. He dresses like a regular person, not someone who flashes his money around. You would never be able to tell his bank account has all those zeros attached to it.

I also don't want to be that woman who gets offended that he never said anything. All I wanted was some truth. Was that so hard?

"Say something, please?" He takes a deep breath. "You haven't let me touch you since dinner. Did I do something wrong?"

"North, I can't have this conversation while you're driving. Take me back to my cabin, please."

"*Fuck*!" he yells as he grips the steering wheel tighter.

I stay silent, afraid of what could happen if I start talking. The last thing I need is for us to get into an accident. When my cabin comes into sight, that's when I feel like I can finally breathe. He parks the truck but never turns it off.

"Talk, Noel. What the fuck is going on?"

I turn to look at him, and his eyes flash to meet mine. "When were you going to tell me?"

"Tell you what? That my family owns the cabin resort? I didn't think it was important, but if this is what it's about—My parents bought it when I was little and kept it even after moving away. Pops couldn't fully retire. This turned into his side project."

God love his dad. I knew someone cared for these with a lot of love and love for Christmas.

"Not the cabins North, about who you are."

He jerks back in his seat and presses his back against the door. "What do you mean, who am I?"

"North Bradford, owner of Bradford Industries. When your dad talked about your multi-million-dollar company, I figured it out and saw your last name on a frame in the hallway."

He doesn't say anything, so I continue.

"You know that oilfield company I work for."

"Please don't, Noel."

"You're my fuckin' boss's boss, North. I slept with the CEO of the goddamn company," I said, catching my breath.

He drops his head into his hands right before he punches his steering wheel. I jump from shock.

"Goddamn it, Noel. Couldn't I have this one week away from all that shit? You were perfect for me, so perfect," his words faded.

"Trust me, North, it was amazing. It was the most fun I ever had. The only thing I wish was different was you. I wish you had told me some truth as to who you are. You didn't have to hide the real you. I told you the worst parts of my life, and you felt you couldn't trust me with your world. Was any of it real?"

I brush away a tear that begins to fall as he sits up and stares out the windshield.

"Noel, I've told my story to so many women only for them to use me." He looks at me with such heartbreak. "I wanted this one time to feel what it was like to be seen for once. I wanted one chance, and fuck, did I love it. Do I regret every time I looked up at you to see your smiling face that I didn't tell you who I was? Yes. Do I wish I could go back and try again? More times than I'd like to admit."

Every breath turns shaky the more he talks. Then, the rage set in.

"You could've still fuckin' told me. Do I look like someone after money or status? I should've said no to you in the first place. I'm sorry about everything, North."

I open the truck door. I don't look at him again. "Merry Christmas." I hop out and slam it behind me. I work my way to my cabin door, trying not to fall. Do not have a breakdown yet, Noel. You wait until he's gone to do that!

Once I'm behind the door, I hear his truck back out of the driveway. I collapse against the door, slowly sinking to the floor.

Add this to another Christmas of memories I'll never forget. Fake dating was supposed to be easy. Where was this in the handbook? That's right. We didn't have one. I get my shit together and head to my room. There's no reason for me to stay until the twenty-seventh. I might as well head home tomorrow and look for a new job.

So much for his coming through his end of the deal because Christmas sucks ass.

20
North

She hasn't said a single word since leaving my parent's house. She keeps looking out the window. The tension between us is building. I can feel it. I finally can't take it anymore, and I need answers because if I did something wrong, I need to know. I can't part knowing I hurt her.

"Say something, please?" I take a deep breath. "You haven't let me touch you since dinner. Did I do something wrong?"

She shifts in her seat and plays with her bag, which makes me even more nervous.

"North, I can't have this conversation while you're driving. Take me back to my cabin, please."

That is not the answer I was looking for. When people say this, it usually means terrible fucking news.

"*Fuck*!" I yell. I grip the steering wheel tighter, causing her to jolt. Perfect. She's probably scared of me now. I've never raised my voice around her before or gotten upset.

Now, my mind is flooded with every single possibility— The second I park, I don't waste any time.

"Talk, Noel. What the fuck is going on?"

I wasn't expecting that or the last words I'd ever hear from her. It probably killed her to say "*Merry Christmas*." The other issue is she blames me for not being honest, but can you blame me?

I've had several women date me for my money and status. As much as I want to trust Noel, I don't know her. We've only known each other for a few days, which is crazy the more I think about it. It feels like I've known her for years, but it doesn't change a thing. She thinks I'm a lying bastard. I wait until she's inside her cabin before backing out of her driveway.

I want to head back to my place, but I feel I will hit up the liquor bottle, which won't end well. I decided a drive might do me better.

I replay everything in my head over and over. The only thing that sticks out is that she works for me in my company building. Out of all the companies in the city, she works at the mine.

I'm still pissed that she's mad at me for not opening up more. I hit the gas pedal, swerving the truck's tail end on the icy road. I thought we had something special. I didn't want this to end. I wanted to exchange contact information and see if we could continue this. I should've known better. Nothing good will ever happen to me in the romance department.

I'm so lost in my thoughts that I don't see the elk run out in the middle of the road until it's too late. I slam on the brakes, only for my truck to swerve across the road. I try to keep it on the road, but the ice has other plans. I slam into the ditch hard, and it sends my truck airborne. I get tossed from side to side, slam into the door, and land upside down. The airbag shoots out now and hits me in the face.

I try to look around but can't see much in the dark. The left side of my face is swollen. It's hard to breathe. I try to move to unbuckle myself, only to receive a jolt of pain across my rib cage. This is going to hurt like a bitch. I try to brace myself as soon as I unclip the seat belt. It's the most ungraceful thing I've ever done. I roll on my back with a groan. My vision fades in and out. The last thing I remember is hissing coming from the engine.

I can feel my body being jostled around, yet I can't get my eyes to open. I can barely see the red and blue lights flash behind my eyelids. Mumbled voices can be heard in the distance, but I still can't seem to find the energy.

"Sir, we have you. You're going to be okay." Some voice calls out above my head.

I try to focus on their words, but my body has other ideas because I fade out again.

My mind has to be playing tricks on me because there is no way Noel is standing in front of me naked, wearing only a Santa hat. I never thought I would be having one of these dreams. I haven't had a sex dream since I was sixteen, the night after I accidentally saw Jenni Murray's breasts for the first time. I thought they were the best thing I'd ever seen, but this, this is the best thing I've ever seen. I watch as Noel silently stalks toward me, never taking her eyes off me.

I want to reach for her, but I'm stuck in the mud. My entire body won't listen to me. I have no choice but to watch. Her hands move along her stomach, working upwards to her perfect breasts. A small groan leaves my lips, not sure if it is in ecstasy or frustration. I open my mouth to tell her to stop teasing, only to find no words will leave me. I'm uncertain if this is a dream anymore. I can only make small groans and grunts.

I watch as Noel approaches my bed. Her hands brush against me, and I feel nothing.

"Wake up, North. Your family needs you now."

Wake up from what? She must be losing it now, not me.

"Now, North."

I watch as she descends from the room, only now taking it all in. This isn't my room at the cabin. I don't know where this room is; I've never seen it before. Everything is blurry and dark. The temperature of the room dips, and shivers rack my body. Alarms start to ring above my head...

Electricity jolts through my body like I've just run through an electric fence at full speed. My heart pounds more quickly than I thought was humanly possible.

Then darkness.

"North, if you can hear me, son. Please wake up. The doctor says it's all up to you now. I get you want to be stubborn, but it's time. Please, son."

The sound of Pop's voice finally wakes me. I only wish my body was prepared for waking up. It's the lights that do me in. My eyes weren't open for a second, and I could hear Pops yelling for a doctor.

"North, can you hear me?" Pops chokes out.

"My eyes are closed. I'm not deaf, Pops," I rasp out. My throat is so dry. It's like swallowing razor blades.

I tug a hand to my throat only to see that it's in a cast.

"You broke your wrist and nose, fractured a few ribs, and have a good old-fashioned concussion. You got lucky, son."

I tilt my head to see him fully. He's sitting in the hospital chair, his greying hair a chaotic mess. Dark bags hang under his eyes, but he still smiles at me. His clothes are very wrinkled, which tells me he hasn't left my side very much.

The doctor finally enters before I can ask Pops where Ma is.

"Glad to see you awake, Mr. Bradford. You gave us quite the fright the last couple of days."

Days? Did he say days? "How many days?" I cough out, and Pops finally hands me that cup of water.

"It's the twenty-eighth. I'm afraid you got smacked pretty hard by the airbag and tossed around really well when you rolled. You probably can leave today once we go over some tests."

"Perfect. Thanks."

I watch him leave, and my eyes are already closing.

"Son, I wanted to call Noel, but I couldn't find her number in your phone."

That had my eyes springing open so much for resting because I was about to crush my Pop's heart. It's a good thing we're in the hospital because I have a feeling he's going to lay me out after I tell him this story.

21

Noel

I spend the entire night packing. If I get home today, I can head to work tomorrow. Then there's less time for me to think about this failed vacation. December hasn't been very kind to me. Thank God it's almost over. Only a few more days and a new year shall begin. I'm only allowing good things into my life. I'm not sure I can deal with any more heartache. I'm afraid my heart will shrivel up and die if I do.

I stare out into the whiteness of the morning. If I'm heading home, I best get moving now. Driving in the winter is not the most fun thing to do. Lucky for me, it's not calling for snow today. It's a little over an hour until I get back to Calgary. I was hoping North would've shown up on my doorstep, grovelling for forgiveness. I shouldn't have expected it. He must not want the trouble dealing with me anymore. I don't either, but I'm stuck with myself.

I was a raging ball of fury the entire drive to the cabins. I didn't bother looking at any of the scenery. I missed so much now that I'm looking around. The landscape is so beautiful; I don't want to leave this place. I get why North's parents moved back. You're far away from the city, but you have all the outdoors at your fingertips. It's perfect, so perfect that I might move here. Canmore is the ideal place to start a bookstore. My mom would be so proud. Maybe I can convince Dad to move out here with me. He needs a change.

As I near the city, I'm already dreading it. I know for a fact my douche of an ex will be banging on my door tomorrow. He's going to demand that I pay for his tires. My anger is already soaring just thinking about him.

My townhouse looks so dull compared to the cabin. I'll even admit that after yesterday I'm almost sad that I don't have a tiny Christmas tree. Maybe North did help me after all. I dig through my bag, looking for the gift from his parents. I cradle the small gift in my hands.

The snowflake wrapping paper is almost too pretty to open. This rectangle box has had my stomach up in knots since yesterday afternoon. I finally tear into the paper with shaky fingers.

Tears impair my vision until they finally fall down my cheeks. I don't know how she knew I needed this, but I'll be forever grateful. I carefully remove the Christmas angel from the box. It's no larger than my palm and made of crystal. I thread my finger between the ribbon and hold it up, so the light shines through, casting small rainbows across the couch.

It's so beautiful; I should've opened it with Ella. I could've told her how much this means to me. I gently place the angel back in the box, thinking of the date North took me on, building snow angels. Every time I see this angel, I'll think of him.

The knock on my door has me jumping. No one knows I'm home. I stay quiet and hope whoever it is will go away.

"Open the fucking door. I know you're home. Your car is in your parking spot." That angry voice I was hoping to avoid is the culprit.

The knocking gets louder. "Open up now, Noel."

I tiptoe to the door. When I peek through the peephole, black, that asshole has it covered with his hand. I have no choice but to open up. I leave the chain lock on and unlock the doorknob.

"What do you want, Johnathan?" I ask as soon as the door cracks open.

His hand wraps around the door, and the chain rattles. "Let me in, baby. I need to talk to you."

The way he says baby makes my teeth clench together. When North says it, I feel like I'm wrapped in a cozy blanket.

"You're not welcome here anymore. You burnt that bridge when your dick landed in Quinn's goddamn pussy," I snap, my trapped feelings finally coming to the surface.

"That's not how it happened. Please let me explain."

I have a feeling I'm going to regret this. I go to close the door, but his hand stays put. "You have to move, or else this is pointless." I would've parked someplace else if I knew he was being a stalker.

With a deep breath, I opened the door to the one person I thought was going to be *the one*. Now when I stare at him, I see nothing, absolutely nothing. I don't know what I was thinking.

"I want to start off with, sorry. I didn't mean for you to find out this way."

"As opposed to what?" I cross my arms, glaring at him. "Because from where I'm standing, that was the end of it. If you didn't receive my message loud and clear, then I can't help you."

He moves closer to me. "Yeah, we received your message. Because of you, we didn't get to go on our trip."

I drop my lower lip into a pout. "I feel so badly that my lying ex and shitty friend couldn't have the perfect Christmas they planned behind my back. I'm truly sorry for you. Now get the fuck out of my place and never talk to me again."

He makes a move to come forward, but his phone rings. Must be his bitch because he digs it out of his pocket. I see she already has him trained. I point to the door without saying another word.

"You're lucky, Noel. I won't stop until I squeeze every penny out of you," he hissed, venom dripping from his words. I watch until he backs out of my door. I don't waste a second locking it behind him.

I know he wants his money back, but I'll never pay it. He can go fuck himself. I should call the cops and report him, but I have no proof, and I did slash their tires. I could end up being arrested. I'm fucked.

I don't sleep a whole lot, and when my alarm clock goes off, I want to smash the shit out of it. The only thing that stops me is that it's also my cell phone. Cell phones are expensive these days. Time to face the music. It'll be like every other day, except now I'll know I'm working for him. Hopefully, he's not in the office today. All I know is that he was returning yesterday. At least, that's what he said.

The office is like it's always been, a bore. It's empty, with most everyone still on vacation. I head to my office, bypassing the executive elevators. Not once have I ever been in them or passed this floor. I've never had a need for it. Now I'm curious about what's up there. Has North always been a few floors above me? When I sit at my desk, all I see is the stupid screensaver with Bradford Industries bouncing around. I double click my mouse to remove it.

Maybe I should've taken another day off work. It's so quiet and boring here today. I don't think it was necessary to come in. I could call Dad. I probably should call him.

As always, he picks up on the third ring.

"Dearest daughter, how're the mountains?"

"Hey, Dad. I'm actually home. I came home yesterday. I'm at work."

He laughs. "Getting paid to talk to the old man, I taught you right after all. What happened? How come you came home early?"

That I don't think I want to talk about. "Just wanted to come home, Dad, that's all. Dinner tonight?"

"I would love that. I'll make your favourite. Now, get back to work. Love you."

"Love you too."

I force myself to focus on my work and not on the guy I left behind, the one I wanted beyond anything in this world. I didn't want our relationship to be fake anymore.

22
North

Leaving the hospital was the best feeling in the world. The second best is walking into my own house back in the city. My parents wanted me to stay behind, but I swear to all things that are holy, if I get coddled one more time over a simple break, I'll lose my shit. I love Ma, but she needs to learn how to give breathing room. If the doctor said I was good to go, then I'm good.

I did, however, stay the night before coming home. I was too tired to leave right after being discharged. I stopped in at Noel's cabin only to find it empty. She left without me telling her how I felt or giving her an apology. I should've told her about the resort, but I'm not sorry about hiding who I was. Now that I know her, she's not at all like the other women I dated in the past.

I hope she can forgive me and listen to my side. I didn't mean to hurt her. I have no way of contacting her except for one. I didn't want to go this way, but I had no other choice.

Stepping off the elevator to my floor, I wave to my receptionist with my good hand. A look of shock overtakes her face.

"Mr. Bradford! What happened? Do you need anything?"

"I actually do. Can you call Noel Tinsley up for a meeting, please?" I continue to my office without looking back.

She'll hate me for this, but I need to talk to her. I only pray that she's at work today. I could pull up her employee record, but I'm not one to turn this into a stalking relationship. I do fancy owning this company without HR raining down on my ass.

A gentle knock gets me excited. She actually showed up. "Come in," I call out.

I damn near lose my breath when she walks in wearing a black pencil skirt and a cream-coloured blouse. She was beautiful in jeans and a sweater, but holy fuck, I might come in my fuckin' suit. When she finally looks up at me, she gasps. I would, too. My face looks like I've been beaten with a baseball bat.

"North, what the hell happened to you?" She rushes over to me, gently cupping my face with one hand. "When did this happen?" Then she reaches for my cast.

"That's what I need to talk to you about. Did you want to have a seat?"

She shakes her head. "Absolutely not. Talk."

"After we talked, I went for a drive. I was driving like a douche and swerved to miss an elk. I rolled my truck and, well, got a few injuries. I just got home this morning. I went by your cabin, but you had already left. I need to say a few words, and I have no other way of contacting you."

She finally takes a seat. She presses her hand to her throat. "North, I was such a bitch to you. I'm so sorry."

"Stop," I jump in before she beats herself up more.

"It's me, Noel. I'm the problem. I hold back. After all, I can't trust women because I think they are only after my money, and I finally see that you aren't. I don't know how to stop thinking like that. It's been that way for years, and it's hard to turn off."

"I also didn't have to jump down your throat. It was just unexpected. What are the odds that you, out of everyone in the entire world, would be my boss and my fake boyfriend?"

I grin at her. "I say pretty good odds, don't you?"

She rolls her eyes. "North, I have to quit. I can't work for you anymore."

"As the owner, I must say it's sad to see you go, but as your future boyfriend..." I walk over to her, weaving my hand into her hair and tugging at it. "I'm glad. I want you to do what you want and not be stuck in a shitty job you don't love."

"Future boyfriend, eh? That escalated quickly, didn't it?"

"I like to seal the deal, and since when have we ever not worked fast?" I lower my face to hers. "Please forgive me?"

"North, you kept two big secrets from me. It's going to take some time for me to trust you again."

My heart sinks to my fuckin' feet. If I only said something sooner. "I understand. Here, I'm giving you my number. Can I take you out on a proper date?" I grab one of my business cards off my desk and hand it to her. When she holds it, I don't let go. "I need an answer, Noel. Please. One date. That's all I'm asking."

"All right. One. That's all."

"Perfect. Text me your address, and I'll pick you up at eight."

She looks down at the card, flicking it around, then grins. "It's so weird knowing who you are after spending so much time with just North."

"If it makes you feel any better, I'm still just North. I only have to wear this suit now."

She fingers the bottom of my jacket. "I'll admit, you look so fuckin' hot right now, even with the busted face." She laughs.

"That's the ego boost I need. Especially now because I have a few meetings to attend."

"I'll text you," she clarifies before standing. I stand back so she can move around the chair, but her foot slips. I catch her before she hits the floor.

"Bubble wrap, Noel. Invest in it." I kiss her forehead before helping her upright.

"Dickhead. Have fun in your meetings." She carefully walks to the door and turns to stare at me. "Thank you for catching me."

"Always."

My heart is in my throat. I thought for sure she was going to send me a text telling me to go fuck a hat or get bent. Our dates in Canmore were different; they were much more laid back. Dates in the city are more stressful, and they shouldn't have to be. I don't need to show off, but I want it to be special. I could only think of one thing; besides, I have to keep up my end of the deal. If I can't get my little Grinch to fall in love with Christmas by the end of tonight, then I can't say I'm jolly, now can I?

As I pull up to Noel's townhouse, I'm almost rethinking the Christmas thing. Yes, I know Christmas is over, but technically, the holidays still happen until the new year. As I climb the stairs to her front door, I take in her neighbour's place. They all have colourful lights on, and then there's Noel's dark, unlit place. The Grinch truly does live here.

I ring her doorbell, still glancing at the lights. When she opened it, I couldn't help myself. "You know, Grinch. It wouldn't kill you to hang some lights." Then I turned and noticed her. I cough from choking on my spit. "Fuck me," I whisper.

"I would hang lights, but you see, this guy I know didn't get me into the Christmas spirit."

Noel is wearing a long, red-sequined dress that could light up the night sky. She dips her hands behind her coat collar and pulls her hair out, looking gorgeous the entire time. I groan out loud.

"Can I help you?" She buttons up her peacoat, covering her body up.

"Yes, but I'll wait."

I'll wait for as long as I need to. "Ready? Because you are going to love where we are headed."

"North, you planned it. I'm sure I'll love it."

I help her to my rental, and she scrunches her nose. "I liked your old truck better."

"Yeah, same, but I can't salvage it. I'm on the hunt for another one. Until then, welcome to the rental."

She would be drooling over this rental if she were like other women. But no, she'd rather I have my truck from the '90s. Wait until she sees my house. She'll love it more than I do.

23

Noel

After sending North my address, I couldn't think. This is the make it or break it. I want to trust him. I also don't want to give in too quickly. I watched the clock until I could finally leave work. My nerves were a complete wreck until the second I walked into my house.

I'm placing the finishing touches on my makeup when my doorbell rings. I grab my coat before opening the door.

"You know, Grinch. It wouldn't kill you to hang some lights." He coughs, then whispers a quiet *fuck me*, one I don't think I'm supposed to hear.

"I would hang lights, but you see, this guy I know didn't get me into the Christmas spirit."

North is wearing the same suit from earlier. It's black slacks and a matching black suit jacket. My non-existent panties would be wet right now, but instead, my inner thighs grow wet when I press them together.

He ends up taking me to the most unexpected place. I honestly didn't think of ever coming here. Well, I didn't ever see the point. It's the festival of lights. I'll even admit it's beautiful.

"Wow, North. It's breathtaking."

"It really is, isn't it?"

I look over at him, only for him to be staring at me. "The lights, dummy, not me."

He shrugs. "I like what I like, Noel." He takes my hand as we walk amongst the lights.

All around us, kids laugh and point at the lights. Other couples walk around cuddled close together. Christmas brings everyone happiness, and I was too blind to see that. I was so focused on the worst time of my life that I let so much pass me by. If North did one thing, he helped me see the pleasure in life again.

I look at him, broken nose and all. He's still smiling away like nothing can bring him down. You still would never know he owns millions. He doesn't appear to be a tightwad like most rich pricks.

"Come, I have more planned." He gives me that sly grin I love so fucking much.

I pull my bottom lip between my teeth and try to stop my thoughts from running through my head. He grips my chin and tilts my head.

"I suggest you stop thinking whatever it is that you're thinking. Otherwise, all these nice folks are going home with a sight they probably don't want to see, and we are getting arrested for indecent exposure."

"If you were a two-pump chump, we wouldn't get arrested." I tease him.

He runs his casted hand up my thigh, through the slit of my dress. Only his fingertips make contact. "Is this what you want, Noel? Because I can make it happen." He cuts his voice lower the further his fingers move up my dress. "No panties? Such a dirty girl. If I went a little further this way..." His fingers moved towards my clit, and I grabbed his arms tight. "Yep, wet as fuck." He presses his fingertip to my sensitive bud. I let out a quiet moan.

"North, we can't do this here."

"I'm not quitting until you come for me." He looks me in the eyes before rubbing my clit. "I want you to fall apart with all these people walking around, looking at all these lights with their families. I want to hear you moan my name when someone walks by. Now be a good girl and come for me."

My fingers pull at his jacket, and he presses a kiss to my neck.

"*Shit*, I'm going to come."

"Not without my name, baby," he whispers in my ear. He rubs faster, and my stomach contracts before I come, moaning his name. He kisses me on the lips before moving away and smiling.

"North, I can't believe we did that."

"Believe it, baby. Now, let's go before it's too late."

I don't know why we would be late. We pull up to a pizza place that's not even busy. If I'm being honest, I'm relieved. I'm peopled out. I don't think I can do a fancy restaurant, nor would I know what to eat there. We are seated by the window facing the street. I slip my jacket off and notice North struggling with his.

"Have you ever broken a bone before?"

When he finally gets off his jacket, he sits. "Oh, for sure. I broke my leg once. James and I were being stupid and tobogganed off the shed roof. That didn't end very well for me. Then I broke my pinky one year playing hockey. Honestly, I've had so many battle wounds; I'm used to it."

"Jesus, North. I haven't even had a stitch, let alone a broken bone." I'm at a loss for words. What a crazy fucker. "I hope you don't do stupid shit now?"

He looks away, scratching his neck. "*No*, I totally don't," his voice laced with sarcasm.

I think about the naked snow angels and his making me come publicly. Mr. Bradford here likes to live on the edge, yet he fiercely guards his heart.

"North, I'll give you one chance. I believe in my heart you're a good guy, and you didn't mean to hurt me. But please, if you have any more secrets, let me know now."

He reaches for my hand. "I swear, I don't have anymore. It was just the two. I'm an open book." His hazel eyes stare into my green without blinking. I believe him. He doesn't seem to give me a reason not to.

When our dinner finally arrived, we spent the time talking and eating. He tells me about how he started his company and why he chose to. For someone twenty-eight, he didn't waste a second getting his foot in the door. I also decided to tell him about moving and opening up a bookstore. He, of course, gave me his business knowledge, and I appreciated it. He also suggested that his Ma help me as she knows the town better than he does, so she would be the one to find the perfect location.

I'm so nervous that I might be doing this. What if I fail and I become a laughingstock? I'll be in debt and in a town that isn't mine. He must sense a shift in my mood.

"Hey, it's going to work out. I can feel it. I think it's perfect. Besides, you hate your job." He smiles. "What boss encourages one to quit?"

"That I'm not sure of, probably a perfect boss. Thank you, North."

"I didn't do anything. This is all you, baby."

I shake my head. "No, for getting me to believe in Christmas again. It's not about the gifts, the lights, or the day. It's about family and making traditions you can share for generations. I want to make naked snow angels with you for years to come, North."

"Smartest decision I ever made. Next time, I'm fucking you in the snow."

I can't help but laugh. "That will be chilly."

"What are you doing New Year's Eve?" he asks, taking my hand to his lips.

"I'm not sure. What are we doing?"

He simply grins.

24

North

It's New Year's Eve, and we are headed back to the cabins. The nice thing about owning the company is you can take time off whenever and take your real girlfriend with you. This time, she's staying with me in my cabin. Everything is working out how it is supposed to. What a crazy week, huh? Every time I look over at her, I fall more and more in love.

"First thing we need to do is make that snow angel," I tell her.

She smacks me in the arm. "No, it's too fucking cold outside. I'm not getting frostbite, so you can get me naked."

"A man can dream, can't he." I park in front of the cabin. Driving with a broken wrist is the worst. I'm already counting down the weeks until I get this thing removed.

Walking inside the cabin feels like home. It's only been two days since I've last been here, but it's where I always want to be. Maybe Noel is on to something about moving out here. Perhaps it is time to get out of the city.

"God, I love this place, North. But your tree needs to come down." She walks over to it, gently touching the ornaments. I walk up behind her, moving her hair away from her neck.

"I like the tree." I stare at it while she turns around.

"Yeah? I like you." Her hands move to my waist. "I also owe you something." She flicks open the button on my jeans.

"Noel, you don't owe me anything. It's not tit for tat."

"No, but I need you in my mouth, North." She works my pants and boxers down my legs before wrapping her hand around my shaft.

"Fuck, Noel. You don't know what you do to me."

She licks me from my balls to tip and strokes me. I wrap my hand in her ponytail when she takes me in fully. I have to restrain myself from fucking her mouth.

She sucks me greedy and fast, making a mess all over her chin. "You have a very talented mouth," I groan. "Fuck, baby, I'm not going to last much longer."

My hips thrust forward, driving my cock further into her mouth. She takes me even deeper as my cum spills down her throat. I moan loudly. "Fuck, Noel."

She pulls back, wiping her face. She smiles at me, but I'm not done with her yet. I remove her leggings and move her to the floor next to the tree. I start by fingering her wet core.

"So wet for me already. Does sucking my cock turn you on?"

"Yes, so unbelievably so." She pushes her hips up. I move my hand under her shirt, but my cast gets caught. I growl.

"Get on your knees." When she gets into position, I lick her wet pussy before lining up. With one deep thrust, I push my cock inside. We groan together.

"Fuck, Noel. Your pussy is so hungry for me." I thrust slowly so I could feel her pussy clenching around my cock. "Do you feel how hard my cock is inside of you? Do you feel your pussy clenching around my cock?" I rock deeper, getting her to moan. "Fuck, baby."

"Come around, my cock." I thrust faster and grab her hips.

"North," she moans.

"Yes, baby. Fuck me."

She rocks her hips into me, and I can feel myself getting closer. "Come for me, Noel. I'm so close." I thrust faster, groaning when she comes. I spill inside of her. "Oh, fuck,"

I moan. I plunge a few more times before I collapse on the floor.

"Shit, that was intense." She lies there all sweaty. I tilt my head to look at her. It's that moment I know for sure I don't want to live another day without her. I roll over her and reach for her present under the tree.

"Here. I didn't have time to give this to you."

"North," she says with a whispery breath. She gently unwraps the present and gasps.

Tears fill her eyes, and then she bursts into laughter. I can't help it; I laugh too.

"Where the hell did you find this?"

"At the market on our date. It's perfect, isn't it?"

She's holding in her hand a Grinch ornament with a sign that says Noel. It was perfect, and I had to buy it for her. She stands and places the ornament on the tree.

"There, the first ornament to our tree."

I stand and wrap my arms around her. "It's beautiful. Maybe this will be our new tradition, finding random ornaments for our tree."

"I love that idea." She turns slightly. "I love you, North."

I kiss her lips. "Noel, I fell in love with you the second you almost smacked me with your shovel."

She winces. "Sorry about that. You did scare me."

"I'm over it. Besides, everything turned out well, didn't it?"

She shrugs. "I do owe your parents an apology. I lied to them and felt like a bag of shit."

For someone who says she doesn't have a heart, she cares a whole lot about others. "No need. I told them about everything. They probably love you more for what you did for me. On the other hand, I ended up in the shit books with Ma. They will be overjoyed with the news that we are no longer fake."

"Still, they are the nicest people. You are fortunate."

That I am.

Once we finally get dressed, we head into town. The town has the best fireworks display, probably better than the city. What more could you ask for? Fireworks, mountains, and the girl that you love. It's a perfect ending to the year.

EPILOGUE

Noel

One Year Later

I can't believe it's been a year, an entire year of North and Noel. It's been a whirlwind, that's for sure. I quit my job eventually because when you're fucking the boss's boss, it doesn't look good if you try to sneak up to the executive floor to see him. After much thought and convincing, Dad moved to Canmore. He was there for Easter, and he fell in love with the place. North's parents also fell in love with Dad. David gave Dad a job helping out with running the Mountain Escape Cabins. He's never been happier.

Now, as for North and me, it gets a little trickier. I sold my townhouse and moved in with North until we figured out where we wanted to live. After a lot of planning, we eventually moved to be with our family. He's had to hire more people, but North can still run his company. For me, I opened my own bookstore

I looked at so many locations that I thought my dream would never come true. I'm proud to say that Joy's Bookshop has been up and running for the last six months and has been incredible. The community is so welcoming to the new shop. I'm happy I did this. I do, however, have to keep North out of here because he likes to get a little handsy with the shopkeeper.

"Noel, where are you?" his voice carries through the shop.

"I'm in the back," I yell at him.

When I turn around, he's leaning on the doorframe, looking sexy as sin. He's wearing jeans, his plaid button up, and that jean jacket. He's been so laid back that I haven't seen him wear a suit in forever. I almost miss it.

"What did you need?" I try my hardest to keep my eyes on his. But they do drift down south.

He clears his throat. "Eyes up, woman. I came to get you for the tree lighting, or did you forget?"

I rumpled up my face. "Shit, I knew I forgot something. I just received a new shipment of books and got a little excited. It's the new mafia romance I was waiting for."

"I forgive you. That's why you have me. Come on, Grinch, let's go."

Yes, he still uses my old nickname, even though I enjoy Christmas this year. I'm enjoying it so much that I'm cooking Christmas dinner for everyone at our place. I know. I can't believe it, either.

After locking up the store, we make our way to the town centre. I'm reminded of the festival of lights last year when we had our public display time. I can't help but smile.

"I know what you're thinking, and unfortunately, it won't be happening this year because our parents are walking this way." He sounds sad when he says it, and I laugh.

"Maybe we can make those snow angels. It's warm tonight."

"Don't tease me, baby. Because I can't handle it if you're teasing me."

"I'm not teasing, full naked snow angels."

He wraps his arms around me and kisses me nice and deep. He dips me low. "I love you."

"I love you too."

He grins slyly at me, and I shake my head. It's that grin that landed us in trouble. So, I know he's cooking something up, but whatever it is, I'm all for it.

THE END

About the Author

Hello, loves! I'm a Canadian romance writer who's all about the steamy and dark stuff. Horror books, movies, and music? Yes, please! I have a little true crime obsession, but I'll just call it research and pretend it's normal.
If you crave love stories that push the limits of lust, trust, and desire, you've come to the right place.

Follow me for exclusive sneak peeks, giveaways, and behind-the-scenes glimpses into my writing process. And if you want to keep up with my latest releases or connect on social media.

Let's dive into the shadows together, darlings.

ALSO BY

A HITMAN'S DUET

MYLES

CARTER

RUSSO MAFIA SERIES

UNBROKEN

UNBEARABLE

UNDENIABLE

STRANGERS OF EASTWOOD

STRANGERS OF THE NIGHT

STRANGERS OF THE TOWN

RAVENWOOD ACADEMY

ATTICUS

www.ingramcontent.com/pod-product-compliance
Lightning Source LLC
Chambersburg PA
CBHW070400200726
48294CB00003B/1015

* 9 7 8 1 9 9 8 9 1 0 0 6 9 *